CIRCUS BULGARIA

Circus Bulgaria

DEYAN ENEV

*Translated from the Bulgarian
by Kapka Kassabova*

Portobello
BOOKS

Published by Portobello Books Ltd 2010

Portobello Books Ltd
12 Addison Avenue
London W11 4QR

The stories in *Circus Bulgaria* were collected and published in the original Bulgarian as
Всички на носа на гемията by Ciela, Sofia, in 2009.

German translations of the stories were published under the title *Zirkus Bulgarien*
by Deuticke im Zsolnay Verlag, Vienna, in 2008.

A CIP catalogue record is available from the British Library

9 8 7 6 5 4 3 2 1

ISBN 978 1 84627 240 0

www.portobellobooks.com

Text design and typesetting by Lindsay Nash
Typeset by Avon Dataset Ltd, Bidford on Avon, Warwickshire

Printed and bound in Great Britain by JF Print Ltd., Sparkford, Somerset

Contents

CIRCUS BULGARIA

Circus 'Bulgaria'

'I JUST DON'T KNOW WHAT TO DO WITH THE LION,' SAID Pacho the lion tamer to Pavarotti on a cold November day. 'I might just shoot him and then it'll be over.'

Pavarotti was a former colleague from their circus years. His name was Pavel, but everyone had called him Pavarotti at the circus because he was a dreadful singer. He used to be a clown, but he had moved with the changing times and now he was a pub owner – if pub is what you'd call his tin shack in the outer suburb of Iliantsi, near the base of the former circus. Pacho often dropped in for a free drink and to chew the fat.

'You're stubborn,' Pavarotti said. 'You must be nuts not to see which way the wind is blowing. There is no more circus art in Bulgaria, get this into your head! How many more years do you need to work that out?'

'Pour me another one,' Pacho said. Pavarotti knew his friend had no money, so it was always on him. But everything had its limits. And anyway, Pacho got drunk on just two or three glasses. He was getting drunk now.

'You ask why I'm stubborn.' Pacho got heated up. 'It's because that's what I do. Because I'm the best lion tamer in Bulgaria. Because without me, this art will die out.'

'So? Who gives a shit?' Pavarotti smiled his cruel clown's smile. 'I was the best clown too, and so what? You need to think about that proposal I told you about.'

Pacho felt he was getting plastered and got up. He put his cigarettes away in the pocket of his old quilted jacket, waved to Pavarotti and stepped outside. A fine sharp snow was cutting across the air like razorblades, and the lion tamer pulled up his collar. Dead or alive, he had to find two kilos of meat for Caesar. And some food for himself, too. Caesar was his family now. His daughters were in Spain, his son in Los Angeles. All three of them were spectacular circus artists – his daughters were acrobats, and his son a juggler.

He reached the wagon which still bore the faded sign 'State Circus', and next to it the more recently painted letters 'Bulgaria'. He unlocked the padlock and went in. He'd spent his life in wagons like this. Caesar got up to greet him, and rubbed his forehead on Pacho's trousers. A handful of hairs hit the floor like sparks. Caesar had started going bald lately. Pacho sat on the bed and put his arms around the lion's big head. He had to find a solution, but his head was all murky, and he felt sleepy and weak. The former circus base in Iliantsi was now entirely filled by warehouses. Only on Pacho's lot of earth were there a couple of wagons and Caesar's cage, covered with a tarpaulin. During the coldest months, Pacho kept Caesar with him inside the wagon.

Pacho had to pull himself together. He had work ahead of him today: find meat for the lion, eat something and have a training session. He also had to light up the stove because the nights were getting colder. The cognac still boomed in his chest and made him prone to speeches. He jumped to his feet.

'Now, look here, attentiiion!'

The lion sat there, and his yellow eyes looked at him with intent.

'I shall deliver my crowning speech. We have a lot of work today, and yet I observe a complete and total lack of discipline. This cannot go on, is that clear? You, Caesar, haven't eaten today. I take this into account and I sympathise. However, this doesn't mean that we'll skip training. You must train daily, I repeat, *daily*, in order to be on top form. We can only take over the world if we are on top form. Right. Where was I? That's right. Now, there is no connection between eating and training. Eating is eating, and training is training. Eating is optional, but training is not. Is that clear? Right. Now, I'll smoke a cigarette because I'm tired of trying to talk sense into you. Then we'll go to the cage and train.'

Pacho sat back on the bed. He was so tired, he didn't even feel like smoking. He lay back and pulled his coat around him. God knows it was cold, his breath came out like steam. Caesar was a handsome lion some years ago. They came to photograph him when they were making the new national coat of arms. So you could say that Caesar was built into the symbol of nationhood itself, he was the foundation of nationhood, so to speak.

Pacho had drifted off. When he came round, it was even colder. The lion was lying down on the old rug in his corner and he gazed at Pacho expectantly. The hands of the old clock on the table pointed at two. Soon it would get dark, November days were short. Pacho got up and shuffled along to Pavarotti's bar.

'Pour me another one,' he said. Pavarotti got him a drink and sat opposite him at the table. He looked at Pacho silently. The cognac warmed up Pacho's chest.

'Did you think about it?' Pavarotti asked. 'The guy is offering a thousand lev. That's enough to get you through the winter, at least. The animal is suffering like this. And you're suffering too. I understand why you don't want to. But think about it – that guy has a house like a palace. He has a ten-acre park…'

Pacho drained the cognac and stubbed out his cigarette.

'All right,' he said. 'Call them.'

Pavarotti snapped into action. He took out his mobile – one of the first models, big, like a brick – and dialled the number, then went into a corner and waited with a strange expression on his clown's face.

'Pavarotti here, from Iliantsi,' he said. 'The owner is ready. When? OK, yes, that's right, he's right next to your warehouses.' Then he tucked his Neanderthal mobile into his belt and turned to Pacho.

'They'll be there in half an hour. You just have to put Caesar in the cage. That's it. And take your money, of course.'

'How are they going to transport him?'

'They'll take care of it, don't worry. They're experienced. Here's another cognac, on the house.'

Pacho drained the cognac and returned to his wagon. He put the collar on Caesar and took him to the cage. Under the tarpaulin it was dark, and the sand was cold and wet.

'You wait here.' Pacho stroked Caesar's forehead. 'And I'll pop outside for a fag.'

Soon, wheels crunched over the gravel and two cars stopped by the cage – a black Audi and a covered Toyota pick-up truck. Two men with slow-moving eyes got out of the Audi. Two more got out of the truck – Pavarotti and a short, broad-shouldered man.

'This is the owner,' Pavarotti started saying to them. 'Give him the money and we'll go. You can take care of it, right?'

'We'll take care of it,' said one of the Audi men, and reached in the pocket of his leather coat and brought out a big wad of notes. He counted out ten notes and handed them to Pacho. Pavarotti pulled at Pacho's sleeve.

'Come on, let's go for a drink. They'll take care of it.'

Pacho tried for one last glimpse of the lion, but he was hiding in the dark and out of view. Pacho went along with Pavarotti. In an hour, they were both completely legless.

'He'll be fine there,' Pavarotti slurred. 'The guy wants to have his own savannah, you know… He brought two wagons of sand from Africa… Caesar will be kept company by antelopes, giraffes…'

Pacho was resting his forehead on the table. From time to time, he took out a hundred-lev note, waved it in the air and bellowed: 'Another cognac!'

Niki-Nikola

OUR CREW RECEIVED THE NEWS AT THREE MINUTES PAST midday, and at a quarter past we were already on our way. The camera operator was one of the best in television. I was confident it was going to turn out well. Ideas were already forming in my mind about the five-minute reportage we were going to shoot. 'Icarus: One Boy's Flight'.

In the outer city suburb of Youth VII, it took us a while to find the right block of flats. In the end, we parked the car and went straight across the open field towards the last high-rises out there. 'Shoot!' I said to the operator. These clumps of mud, these unfinished concrete alleys buried under piles of rubbish, these old newspapers flying towards us, this rotten mattress, this old stove branded 'Dream' – well, all this could be an excellent backdrop to the opening credits.

Block number 712 turned out to be the highest in the complex. The building greeted us with the slap of laundry on balconies and windows flashing like mercury, with the sky reflected in them. It towered above us at a mind-numbing height. 'Shoot!' I said to the operator, and he turned his camera up to take in the endless rise of the wall.

In the lift, the floor numbers changed with exasperating slowness. We got off on the top floor. 'Shoot!' I said to the operator, and he shot the dark corridor, the cobwebbed heating pipes, the sad flowerpots on the landing. Then we rang the bell.

Niki-Nikola himself opened the door. He shook our hands and invited us in. Not that there was much to go in to. Two steps is all it took to be in the centre of the only room.

'Sit down,' Niki-Nikola said, and we sat around the table. A young woman with deep brown shadows under her eyes sat there. Her face was calm and dreamy.

'I called you,' Niki-Nikola said, 'so you can film my flight. Yesterday I completed the construction of my wings. I made them according to the classical method – from resin and feathers. I am seven years old, for your information. In my short life I have never left this room. I have studied the history of human civilisations in great detail. After long reflection, I have concluded that there is no real reason why humans shouldn't be able to fly. That's what I say. I intend to demonstrate this with my first attempt, and without further ado. This is my mother.

She can second my words.'

The camera was buzzing quietly. The woman moved for the first time now.

'Niki-Nikola is mature enough to be accountable for his actions,' she said. 'Everything he says is true. I support his brave enterprise. Niki-Nikola and I have established that it's not gravity, but fear that stops people from flying. I trust that my son will prove this.'

Niki-Nikola was already standing in the middle of the room, waving his arms up and down.

'I'm warming up,' he explained. 'My muscles have to be warm for this.'

When he'd finished his warm-up, he pulled out the wings from underneath the bed.

'The feathers come from pigeons,' the mother said quietly. 'We get lots of pigeons on our window sill. Still, it took us half a year to collect enough feathers.'

Niki-Nikola strapped the elastic onto his arms and the big wings moved the stale air in the room.

'OK,' he said, 'I'm off.'

His mother opened the window and he stepped up on the sill. The operator pointed his camera and shut his eyes. His camera was working.

Niki-Nikola pushed off with his feet. The operator rushed to the window and continued shooting.

The reportage was aired the same day on Channel One and it was a success.

Its title was as I'd planned it, 'Icarus: One Boy's Flight'. The ending was especially good. It included a two-minute interview with the mother.

'I couldn't stop him from doing it. We spent so many years shut up in this tiny room, just the two of us. It was terrible. Nothing good awaited us down there either, just clumps of mud. You know, we had so much fun collecting the feathers. You are mistaken if you believe that Niki-Nikola is dead. My boy is far away now, very far away. He flew away to another country, where people are not afraid.'

From the Life of Hedgehogs

Krum Vassev stood by the window. There was a full moon tonight. It kept growing until it became larger than its own metaphor. Then Krum knew he had to go out and see people, one person at least. The full moon was merciless to loners.

He put on his coat and stepped outside. When the wind put out his match for the third time, he gave up trying to light a cigarette. Most of the houses in his little street were lit up, but for a long time now the sculptor had had no access to any of them. At the end of the street he spotted a small figure. It gave him the illusion that he had a purpose tonight. His hackles went up – for a long time now he'd feared human company, and also desired it desperately. The little figure at the end of the street was strangely insubstantial, not quite grown-up. When he drew closer, Krum saw that it was a boy. The boy took little notice of Krum. He was listening out for something.

'Hi,' Krum said, and managed to light a cigarette. He drew on it and tried to look casual.

'Hi,' the boy said. 'Can you keep quiet, please.'

'Why?' Krum had already forgotten about being casual.

'I'm hunting for hedgehogs,' the boy explained. 'On a full moon, there are always lots of hedgehogs. I had a hedgehog at home once. He was a character. He kept poking his snout in the kitchen. But you know, it's a lie what they say about hedgehogs, that they can dance to music. It's not true at all – in fact, they can die from it.'

'So do you sell them?' Krum asked. He was fully absorbed by the fact that here he was, like a normal person, walking and talking with someone who didn't want to get rid of him straight away.

'No, why would I sell them? I let them go. They're hilarious. They walk just like people, tap-tap. But it's rotten to keep them shut indoors. I kept mine in the basement and he lost five kilos.'

Krum puffed on his cigarette with pleasure, letting out ringlets of smoke. He was just enjoying the mild evening, the mysterious breeze, the shadow-spotted street.

'Apparently some people tame them,' he ventured. 'They give them custard and teach them to wear hats.'

Krum was trying to sound knowledgeable but really, he was talking rubbish. He looked at the boy to check if he realised how clueless Krum was.

'Why would you do that?' the boy asked seriously. 'I can always catch a hedgehog if I need one. But you really mustn't keep them shut in. What if they have a family?'

Krum shut his eyes and walked like that for a moment. He suddenly thought of his ex-wife. She'd written to say they'd settled in. Her boyfriend Bobi was now sculpting tombstones, and she sold Coca-Cola in some fast-food joint. Bobi had been Krum's best friend. They went to university together, they sold their first sculptures together. They thought it would always be like this: the life of the bachelor, the life of the artist. In their visions of the future they saw a big studio, where they'd work together and throw parties to celebrate their joint successes. They would be this luminous, inseparable twosome. Then Krum got married. Bobi took it philosophically, saying that from now on they'd be an inseparable threesome.

Krum gave a start. The boy had bolted across the empty field, his running figure lit up by the moonlight. The tall grass hissed and closed in small concentric circles behind him.

So Bobi was making tombstones in a provincial Danubian town. And the ex-wife brought him Coke, to keep him cool in the summer heat.

Damn it, the full moon was doing his head in.

The boy came back after a while. He held something in his hands.

'Look at him,' the boy said. 'He thought he was going to run away.'

The hedgehog was surprisingly big. Underneath the spikes, Krum could see his little snout poking out, just like in hedgehog illustrations.

'You're pretty good at this, aren't you,' Krum said with sincere admiration. 'How did you hear him in that grass?'

The boy shrugged modestly. It's not a big deal, the shrug was meant to say, but there was pride in it too. Then the boy said: 'Do you know the sculptor? The one who lives here and whose wife ran away?'

'I know him,' Krum said slowly. 'What about him?'

'Nothing. Dad says he's got real talent, but he's always drunk. His wife drove him nuts. But Dad says, no matter how cut up we are, we must always pick ourselves up. Especially people with talent.'

Krum didn't say anything. He kept trying to light another cigarette but the wind wouldn't let him.

'Dad said that apparently his wife wanted to marry the Beatles, because there's four of them. But the sculptor said, why not marry a folk choir, there's even more of them in it.'

'She wasn't a bad person,' Krum said.

'Did you know her?' The boy suddenly fixed his gaze on

him with interest.

'Yes. I've seen her. She was very beautiful. The problem was, she loved to dance. All night long. And she wanted others to dance with her, and she turned the music right up. That was the problem.'

'Look at him,' the boy said. He'd let the hedgehog down and the creature was now sniffing his trainers. He picked it up and together, Krum and the boy headed back across the field, diving in and out of deep moonlight shadows. Eventually they returned to Krum's street.

'Are you going to let him go?' Krum asked.

'Yep. I just catch them for fun. Then I always let them go.'

'Isn't he going to be lost, though? What if we got him too far from his family?' Krum fretted.

'Don't worry. I'll take him back to where I found him. I always do that. Hedgehogs are very sensitive. If they get lost, they can become depressed. OK, I'd better go. See you!'

'See you,' Krum said. He tried for another cigarette, but the sudden wind overpowered him again.

'If you like, I can take you with me next time, just let me know,' the boy shouted.

'OK, I'll let you know,' Krum said quietly. And suddenly he realised that he was standing outside his own door. He'd never taken this route before. He'd hacked a special path across the shrubs, and he usually came and went that way. For some reason, unlocking the rusty padlock of his door filled him with delight. And just before he fell asleep, he thought: 'Of course they don't dance. Even the sound of music is enough to kill them.'

The Small Orange Spot in the Distance

TODAY IS AN IMPORTANT DAY, PERHAPS THE MOST IMPORTANT in my life so far. I got up early and shaved. I asked for a fresh pair of pyjamas. And without delay, I went out on the terrace to wake up the pigeons. Come on, my birdies, go and bring me some news.

The alleys in the small hospital park were dark like gun barrels. The dawn glittered here and there among the shrubbery. Beyond the park and its noiseless silver foliage, the city was beginning to roar.

Today, my son is turning four. Good morning, Daddy's little dewdrop, good morning.

Now crack on, my birdies, and bring me some news.

I quickly inhaled two cigarettes in the frosty air. The hours will stretch out endlessly until lunchtime, when I'm allowed to smoke again. As you have correctly guessed, smoking is prohibited here.

After the doctor's visit, I tried to sleep a bit. They don't make as much fuss about me any more. This time they just came in, asked about my dreams and left. Their faces were impenetrable. So there's not much else left to do except sleep. Sleep until the next cigarette. Then, for a second, life will flare up and burn inside my chest.

I must have nodded off. Suddenly, a pebble hit my window. Then another one. I calmed my breathing and thanked my birdies. I got out of bed slowly, like a man who was indifferent to it all. But I wasn't. I saw them instantly: my two beloved heads. The third one wasn't there. I put on my gown and went out on the terrace. Mum's face was ridiculously calm. My son looked a bit startled, like a teddy bear with buttons for eyes.

'Hello there, Daddy's little dewdrop,' I said. 'Hello Mum.'

Then I didn't say anything. Mum wasn't saying anything either.

'Happy birthday to Daddy's little dewdrop!' I then said, in a grand, official way to match the occasion. 'From today, you will be a grown-up man. When I was four, you know…'

The iron railing between us really bothered me.

'Hang on,' I said, 'I'll come over.' And I jumped over it.

I could see Mum twitch with worry and shelter the boy.

'I'm not contagious, you know,' I felt like yelling, 'I'm not bloody contagious!' But I didn't. I managed to stifle the savage cooing deep inside my belly.

'I brought you oranges,' Mum said, as we hurried off to the most private alley in the park. My boy had run ahead, so I said: 'Where's Veronica?'

'Working. The experiment failed, and they're working round the clock.'

'Aha. Fine. And how are you?'

'Fine. Spending time with Tsetso. You know, he's so clever, he's already talking.'

I pretended I didn't see Mum's shrewd little trick: she was walking along an imaginary straight line, exactly two metres beside me. I pretended this loud conversation was the most natural thing in the world.

'Aha,' I said.

My son had explored the shrubs and was now running back to us.

'Dad,' he said, 'there's a tiger in there. I saw him.'

In child's language, he was announcing to me that when he is with me, he is not afraid of anything. How I wished for a tiger now, the biggest tiger in the world to come out of the shrubs. I would put him in a headlock with my big strong arms.

Out of the shrubs came a striped cat. He looked at us with contempt and moved on. Daddy's little dewdrop was watching me, making sure I wasn't afraid. I returned the cat's look of contempt. My son's eyes filled with jubilation, and this was enough for me. I took out a cigarette and put it in my mouth. Mum looked at me in quiet horror.

'Pass them over,' I said, and moved the fingers of my right hand. And, still looking horrified, she reached inside her handbag and took out two packets of cigarettes. Suddenly, Daddy's little dewdrop stood before me.

'Dad, why do you smoke?' he said severely. 'Mum said it's all because of the cigarettes. Your bloody cigarettes, she says.'

'She's right,' I said. 'Your mum is right. Except, you know…'

And I looked at my birdies, which were decorating a nearby tree. So, it's the cigarettes, Veronica says. But Veronica, we smoke to lighten our memories.

How I wanted to give my son a bicycle. I would get on my old bicycle too, and we'd pedal together, pedal together. It is terrible when it's your son's birthday, and you are unable to celebrate.

The pigeons were following me with their eyes. Mum was peeling orange after orange, placing the segments on a newspaper spread out on the grass and discarding the orange peel in a little heap. And suddenly, something flared up in my mind. I'd seen it from my window: a little orange spot at the end of the alley, near the fence of the park's grounds.

'Come on, Daddy's little dewdrop.' My son came trotting after me, full of blind trust.

It was, as I had suspected, an electric forklift. They'd used it to shift the piles of dry leaves. Its square orange snout promised adventures.

My green hospital gown instantly turned into a cracked old leather jacket. A pair of huge celluloid eye-shields fell over my eyes. My son was observing this transformation with fascination. It was only when we'd got into the seats that I realised the machine was turned off. The little person was shivering next to me. The wind of great adventure was already playing with his hair.

I'd driven an electric forklift once upon a time. All I needed now was a sharp stick to make it go. But my son mustn't see this. God, don't let him see this. He was turning four today. Four-year-olds believe in their fathers, that their fathers can start up and drive an electric forklift. I reached into the pocket of my gown. Of course they can. I felt a little serrated blade inside my pocket – one of those used to cut glass ampoules. I inserted it in the ignition and turned. The engine roared to life. I turned it around and drove it straight down the alley. The wind of great adventure blew in our faces.

My two darling men, Veronica used to say, you are impossibly identical. I look at one, and I see the other.

I went round the bend like a professional. Dry leaves flew everywhere. The tyres whistled. We squinted with our identical eyes. Our identical lips were clenched, as you expect from heroes perpetually living on the edge.

The pigeons flew off somewhere behind us. We were flying faster than them.

The trees became blurred, like two uninterrupted lines on each side of us. The details disappeared. There were no more pebbles, benches, shrubs, no more landscape. Just the distance – inviting and seemingly within reach. I was in a hurry. I had to show him many things. I had to answer all his questions. All the questions he would ask in the future. Our moment had to be long enough to fit in all of this. Our beautiful, orange moment.

Please God, teach him how to look for the little orange spot in the distance.

And now, Daddy's little dewdrop, we have to stop, before they catch us. Such is the code of honour of men who live perpetually on the edge.

Surprises, of course, are always just around the corner. When I returned the forklift to its spot, a man in blue overalls was waiting for us. I stared at him intimidatingly. If he were made of paper, he would have burst into flames. We got off the vehicle, and the man's features suddenly softened.

'Good afternoon,' I said politely. 'Why haven't you cleaned the machine properly?'

'Sorry, boss,' said the man indulgently. 'Tomorrow everything will be fixed. Don't you worry.'

We headed back towards Mum. My son was walking beside me, his hands in his pockets. This was enough for me. It meant that his father was the strongest of all.

They saw me off along the alley, I jumped back across the iron railing and waved to them from my terrace.

'We'll do it again tomorrow, right Daddy?' my son said.

'Sure thing,' I said.

I looked at him carefully. There were no tears in his eyes. He was a four-year-old man. This was the look of a man who knows the price of tomorrow. And the price of memories, which is the same thing.

I looked at Mum too. She was splendid about the whole thing. She smiled.

'And kiss your mum from me,' I said to him.

'OK, Daddy.'

'And be good and listen to your mum.'

Isn't it amazing, Veronica, when there is someone in this world who looks like you?

From the far end of the alley, my son waved. Mum waved too. Then they went around the corner. The corner always looked like a bracket.

Before I went back into my room, I checked that the orange spot was still there. Till tomorrow, I muttered, and almost believed myself.

Come on, birdies, where are you? We can coo now all we like. We might even fly a bit. Just a bit, enough to get used to the chill up there, in the sky.

The Marionette

HER STRUGGLES LASTED HALF A YEAR. AT THE END OF THE summer, some friends suggested she try in a bar – after all, she had nothing to lose. Meanwhile, she kept rehearsing with the puppets. After much consideration, she'd called them Tiberius and Belinda. Fantastic names for puppets, don't you think?

Zornitsa Popova was accepted into the Academy for Film and Theatre at the age of twenty. She'd had a lonely childhood, with dolls for company. So after finishing high school, she decided to go back to her dolls. At the end of her degree, she received a diploma with a beautifully inscribed 'Marionettist' on it.

After six months of unemployment, her savings had melted away. In her room, the marionettes would look at her with their huge eyes. She would nod at them, have tinned sardines for supper yet again and sit down with the French language book, to stop herself wailing with despair. Her lecturer at the Academy had mentioned that the best language for marionettes was French. It was only later at night, when Tiberius and Belinda were asleep, that Zornitsa would cry. They were very sensitive, and her tears unbalanced them easily.

So she tried the nightclubs. The managers would just look at her in alarm and turn her away. Whoever imagined puppets in a nightclub? Then, one day, a new hotel was officially opened in the capital. This was her last chance.

The hotel's director was young and energetic. He welcomed her idea with interest. They didn't go as far as to sign a contract, but he promised to see what he could do for her and her marionettes. She gave him her number.

The following day, she took them out for a walk to celebrate this hopeful new development. Tiberius and Belinda asked to be taken to the South Park, and so she did. She bought herself a juice, and ice cream for the marionettes. Tiberius made a complete mess of it and Zornitsa reprimanded him, in French of course. But her French was still not up to scratch, and Tiberius gave her a look of contempt. Then another blow came when Belinda decided that she wanted to be naughty too, and the walk concluded with both of them falling into the lake. Zornitsa was beside herself with anger. She took them aside to a rotunda in the park and sat them down. She tried to study French from her book. But they wouldn't let her – now they started to hiccup and complain of the sun shining in their eyes. Zornitsa made them apologise by lifting them up on their strings. Tiberius shook her hand apologetically, and Belinda curtseyed. In the evening, they had omelette and Coke. Then they all kissed goodnight and slept like babies.

The next day, the young director of the new hotel called her. He said he had an idea, and was she free after five? She said she normally had her French lesson with the marionettes then. The young director laughed a grainy, manly laugh on the phone. They made a time to meet up anyway.

The marionettes were asleep and didn't hear anything, which was just as well. She didn't want to worry them. She took out her sewing machine – a present from her grandmother – and by lunchtime she'd managed to make herself a new white skirt. She tried it on with a light yellow blouse, and when she saw herself in the mirror, her heart beat faster. The marionettes looked at her suspiciously. Zornitsa reassured them that it's a business outing, it's not what they were thinking, and if she was late tonight they must go to bed like normal people and not stay up all night. She said all this in excellent French. The marionettes promised to be good. She kissed them goodbye – Tiberius on his bristly moustache, Belinda on her blond tresses – and locked the door behind her.

In fact, she had a whole hour before her rendezvous. She walked around a bit, to get used to being in the world like this.

She even had a coffee. With every passing minute she felt more confident. At first, it was a random male gaze. Then a truck full of young army recruits bellowed at her like they were about to attack. Then three old geezers, their blood warmed up by the afternoon sun. And finally, some hapless youth with sunglasses. In the city centre the crowds were denser and the male looks more intense, and Zornitsa walked among them, her white skirt stroking her legs pleasantly.

The young director had reserved a small table for two with a view over the square. His thick, wheat-coloured moustache and well-shaved, bluish chin reminded her of the musketeer-like charm of chivalry. It had been so long. They drank two cocktails each, then another two. The cold daiquiri went right into her soul and the breeze of hope blew over her. The director was a man of his word. Though, he said, he didn't exactly have a magic wand. She would start on a probation period of two weeks. During that time, she'd have to work out her repertoire according to the rest of the night's programme because, after all – and he smiled bitterly – art is art and the public is there to be entertained, and if you didn't take that into account as an artist, well, you were a loser, weren't you. This didn't mean that his nightclub was vulgar in any conceivable way. Not at all, on the contrary – it was the bar's special opening hours and the clientele's particular disposition that could create the right environment for the artist.

The main issue here was timing, he said. Puppet theatre was a great idea, by the way, what with the usual diet of magic, cabaret, pop, acrobatics and a dash of humour – which is the standard fare at any nightclub, under any director…

Zornitsa listened and agreed with everything. The daiquiris, the tender September evening, the nobly greying temples of this young director – all this had found its way into her heart. She felt at peace, the way you do after feeding pigeons in the square.

In the sudden darkness that fell over the city, secret signs and lights appeared.

Ah, the night, she thought – the night revealed that which was beautiful, and concealed that which was not. Clusters of human voices soared towards the sky. Couples walked like entwined coral. And there was the sound of steps everywhere. There are so many fates, like mine, Zornitsa thought, and that of my marionettes. So much suffering over this last half-year. But then who was she to claim a monopoly on suffering, when right here next to her there was a woman missing half her face, drinking gin through a straw. And that old man over there – the great wise pedestrian of Sofia who criss-crosses the city all day long with his white biblical beard and a bag over his shoulder, and disappears into the darkness every night, to be reborn in the morning – what terrible blow of fate had swept his life away? Or the little crowd of deaf-mutes sitting at the next table – they too are drinking, and their tongues are getting thick with alcohol, thick to bursting. But no words will ever come out.

The darkness splintered as if struck with a fist, and again Zornitsa was sitting opposite the wheat-coloured moustache, the pleasant tan and the warm eyes of the director.

'Hello, where are you?' he was saying.

'Oh, I was checking if the marionettes were asleep,' she said.

'Everything all right?'

'Yep, they're sleeping.'

'OK, so it's a deal. In a couple of days, you'll introduce me to those two – what were their names? Tiberius and Belinda, right?' The director looked at his watch, and at that very instant the waiter materialised by their table.

'And now, I have something for you,' he said. They were walking along the pavement and she held him by the elbow. 'I'm taking you to a club. Not our one, of course, that would make you nervous. Just a club, so you can see for yourself.'

His manly elbow led her with such confidence that turning him down wasn't an option. Would Tiberius and Belinda like him, she wondered? They never liked the men she went out with. But this one's different. They would understand. Then she thought of Tiberius's bristly little moustache, his pride and joy, and glanced at the virile, hirsute accessory of the director.

The entrance of the club was crowded, but the doors opened wide for the director. A young man in a black dinner jacket showed them down the stairs. At the door of the club, which gaped open before them like a rumbling red cave, stood the manager himself. He was heavyset but had handsome nocturnal wrinkles down his cheeks. He took them to the best table, sat with them for a minute, then wished them a pleasant night and disappeared like a genie. The orchestra played pleasant golden oldies. Two whisky glasses appeared on their table as if by magic. The ice cubes had little bubbles of air inside them. This was the best ice in the world, the director explained, from Greenland, for special guests only. This ice was formed in ancient glaciers, and so the bubbles of air inside it belonged to another era altogether. So when the ice melted inside the whisky, it released the flavours of ancient times. Zornitsa sipped the whisky reverentially.

Suddenly, two red projectors split the club in two. Four girls ran along the beam of red light. The stares of the men hardened the air, but even so, the girls' bodies glowed softly as they floated about. They were all moving in identical ways, and their bodies were almost identical too – their shoulder blades were delicate like sea-horses' wings and their hips were narrow like a needle's eye. Zornitsa thought how these girls were just like the bubbles of air inside the ice cubes – delicate and unfree in the space provided for them. They couldn't take a single step outside their choreographed routine. The orchestra's instruments flashed in the reddish darkness, pointing towards the girls' limbs like barely visible strings. The girls disappeared the way they had come – down the path of red light. The director didn't give them the time of day, even though they fluttered around his table the most. His only acknowledgement was the crunching of ice cubes between his teeth. He urged Zornitsa to have some more almonds.

Next, the projectors cast a yellow spot of light on the stage the size of a coin. A man in coat-tails appeared, took out a box the size of a dominoes box, turned it this way and that and started extracting alarm clocks from it. Out they came, one after the other, until he'd got twenty of them. But it wasn't enough. He handed it over to one of the patrons and the man cried out in amazement – the box really was empty. Then the man in the coat-tails extracted another twenty alarm clocks. You could count them at your leisure – he was arranging them on a surface covered in black velvet. When he got bored with the alarm clocks, he crumpled the box and turned it into a gorgeous silk handkerchief. And from the hanky he started removing walking canes, like the ones gentlemen used in the belle époque of the city. One of the canes found its way to Zornitsa, and she held it without breathing, in case the spell was broken and everything vanished. But the cane was real – long, hard and shiny. In the musical intermission after the magician, Zornitsa met the director's eyes. He smiled condescendingly.

'I can only say one thing.' He leaned towards her. 'One of the canes is real. But you don't want to know how it fitted into the hanky, do you? Magic is the last fairy tale of the twentieth century. Why ruin it?'

The director took a sip of his whisky and focused on the two gladiators on stage. One of them was an old wolf, his pectorals absurdly prominent and his back the size of a horse-carriage, while his thighs were startlingly narrow. The other was still a boy, with the body of a stag and fine, amber-coloured skin. They did a few acrobatic numbers, but the beauty was in the movement of the bodies. There was so much harmony in those tensing muscles, coloured in turn blue, yellow or green. Their eyes were closed as if they were in a trance. The director's voice startled her out of her reverie.

'Unfortunately, too much male beauty gives rise to its polar opposite,' he said enigmatically. 'But what do we care?'

Zornitsa took a rather large gulp of her whisky, and her teeth clanked against the glass. It was only now that she noticed the gold rings on each of the director's hands. The programme ended with the same four girls. Zornitsa looked at their faces this time – they were disconnected from the graceful bodies, frozen in a static smile like a mask that protected them from the heavy red air, the hands of the men, the alcohol which made reality and fantasy one and the same. And again, Zornitsa saw those invisible strings and she had a realisation. But it was so absurd and horrible she didn't dwell on it, and tried to forget it immediately.

The air outside was fresh and cool, like mountain air. They got into one of the taxis waiting outside.

'Eagles' Bridge,' the director instructed the driver.

The taxi dropped them off in front of a building with a wide black marble staircase. The director unlocked the aluminium door and it clicked shut behind them. The black marble went on inside his apartment, and led to a lovely polished wooden floor decorated with fluffy rugs. All around her, as in a dream, Zornitsa registered dark surfaces and screens. Then a discreet lamp came on, light like a fragrance. Zornitsa's ankles suddenly touched a low bed, vast as a meadow. Later, the tinkle of early-morning trams came through the open windows.

Two days later, Methody received her and the marionettes in his office. Tiberius and Belinda were amazed to find that he didn't even glance their way.

'Right,' he said. 'The first night is up to you. Just don't forget that a club is a club.'

They parted like old friends – matter-of-fact and without unnecessary niceties.

Zornitsa's debut in the club came and went like a bad dream. She was a nervous wreck beforehand. Tiberius and Belinda looked down in the dumps as well.

Around five o'clock in the afternoon, she managed to get a grip on herself. She dressed in an austere dark dress with a white collar, like a schoolgirl. Tiberius and Belinda had to make do with ugly children's clothes. Their short play was entitled *The Exam*. Before they left for the club, Zornitsa kissed them and told them it was going to be all right. They kissed her back and muttered something in French.

Her number was after the magician, during the downtime when the patrons of the club can have a drink and chat among themselves. She was untangling the strings when they called for her. She was alone on the stage with the marionettes. The red lighting didn't help at all – it showed up Tiberius's hunchback and Belinda's bow legs. After the first minute, she realised she was a mess of nerves. The marionettes too weren't doing things right. Seen from the side, they were waving their limbs this way and that, their heads were lolling about drunkenly and there was no sense to it at all. Zornitsa was struck with horror.

Her time was up and she retreated to the green room. The marionettes looked like they had hanged themselves on their strings. The old magician gave her a cigarette. She lit up and started coughing at once. Somewhere in the first row of tables she'd glimpsed a little mysterious light, but she was too wrecked to think about it now.

She didn't catch up with Methody that night, or the day after. She had to call him herself. He didn't receive her in his office this time, but downstairs, in the hotel car park. They stood in the entrance to the car park, and Methody lit a cigarette with his expensive lighter.

'It's not looking good,' he said. He didn't look angry or disappointed, he was just stating a fact. 'We have to come up with something else. The art director of the club's programme is totally against you. I had to vouch for you. Look, you have to understand that people are just sitting in their armchairs, quietly drinking and chatting, and you have to get their attention somehow. How? Well, here's the thing. In the art of night performance, there's no relativity. It's all very black and white. Your outfit, for instance – that schoolgirl dress is absurd. I'll have to come up with something else.'

The next night, Zornitsa felt a bit numb. The only thing that surprised her was the outfit Methody had for her, but she knew that in this business there was no going back. This time when she turned up on the stage, the club went quiet. Tiberius and Belinda were obedient and bland and did their job. There was applause at the end.

Back in the green room, one of the waiters walked past and gave her a good once-over.

'You're a bit of a looker, you know,' he said. 'Why don't you chuck these stupid dolls and join the cabaret? They'll snap you up like hot cakes. Pretty girls aren't that easy to find.'

The sweaty stains under his arms smelled of deodorant.

Later that night, Methody came to her room. He was drunk and handsome, dressed all in white. He had two bottles. Zornitsa got drunk. Methody repeated the waiter's words.

'You're so lovely,' he was saying in the dark. 'Drop the dolls and join the cabaret. Look at them, they're just two rag dolls. You're paying a high price for your youth.'

Zornitsa looked at her marionettes and suddenly, she saw that he was right – they were just two dolls made from rags.

A few days later, she went to the cabaret rehearsals. The modern dance classes she'd taken at the Academy for Theatre and Film came in handy now.

Three months later, she was the new star of the cabaret show. She changed her name from Zornitsa – which meant dawn – to Zina, which meant nothing but sounded good. Zina Popova, it had a ring to it. She didn't see Methody any more. Now she was courted by an aged gentleman with a goatee and a rose in his buttonhole. He liked to watch her dance, and whenever he was there, Zina saw a light flash in the first row of tables.

Sometimes, in the late morning when Zina applies her face mask, she tries to talk to her marionettes in French. She is still sleepy at that time, and sad, without knowing why. She kneels in front of them, but they are mute. Then she gets a grip on herself and realises this is all ridiculous, and she gets on with preparing her face mask. How could you ever expect two rag dolls to speak French?

Wedding

STANA VARLACHKA HATED ALL THAT WAS MALE. NO ROOSTER ever crowed in her yard. She destroyed thistle wherever she saw it, as if it was the plague – she cut it with her own hands, piled it up and burned it on a pyre. If she saw a man in the street, she'd turn her head away and spit for a long time. Her household consisted of a she-goat and a couple of hens, that was all.

Along the steep cobbled street, the old village houses were being demolished and new ones built – bright and shiny, with brick façades and big windows. The old people gradually died off. The young lived in the big town and only returned at weekends, unfolded cheerful garden tables and sat around drinking beer. Only Stana never changed. Her adobe house was like a pumpkin stubbornly rooted in the ground. Her messy yard was small like an ox's footprint. There was room for a couple of rows of peppers and a few stalks of onion – that was enough for her. And in the middle of the tiny yard was a rubbish dump – a nice, ripe dump forty years old. Every single day Stana went around the village and dragged back whatever loot she could find – caved-in wicker baskets, old rags, discarded mattresses. She piled on the rubbish, then stood to one side and laughed at something only she knew about.

Stana was ten when the King died in 1943. All the schools had a week's holiday. Stana went off with her mate Zlatko to pick berries. He lived in a nearby neighbourhood. That day, Stana had put on a little necklace of red beads. Who knows why, but that day Zlatko didn't pick a single berry, while Stana managed to fill her bag with them. On their way back to the village, they ran into two gendarmes who'd been drinking. They took the children back with them to the police station. They cracked Zlatko's head, and after two months of agony he managed to pull through. And Stana? They took her into the guards' barracks and left her there overnight. In the morning, some open-shirted sergeant dragged her along to the stables where the municipal bull dwelled. He tied her up in the bull's stalls, and that's where she remained for three days. When they finally let her go, Stana didn't know where she was any more.

The only thing that ever got to her from then on was her parents' deaths. She barely survived them. She had grown up around them – quiet and a little slow. She was content to weave

38

with her spindle in winter, pick at the earth in spring and collect rubbish. It was as if time couldn't touch her. People remembered her as she always had been – small and bony, wrapped in a rough black cardigan with her big, froglike mouth and her thick spectacles that made her eyes blurred and squinty. When she was left all alone in the world, social welfare gave her sixty lev a month, enough to buy bread, salt and – well, that was about it.

Every day the goatherd came by to pick up Stana's she-goat for the day. Stana would tie Bucha to her little gate and hide inside the house. The herd rattled up the street, grazing on shrubs as they went. Ahead of them went the goatherd – green-eyed, limping and broad-shouldered like some wood spirit, a whistle in his mouth. When the noise faded, Stana would come out of the house, her hands would slowly unlock their nervous grip and she'd start picking at the earth – the peppers, the onions. Her glasses glittered in the sun. Then she went off on her rubbish rounds.

At sunset, Stana was back to greet her goat. But today, the herd was late. The sun went down behind the pine forest and a smell of damp grasses filled the air. The herd wasn't coming. Stana's glasses flashed in the sunset as if they were on fire. Panic rushed into her simple soul. Then suddenly, she heard a distant tinkle. It grew closer, until a cloud of dust appeared at the top of the street. The herd flowed down the street and into the open front-yard gates. As usual, the male goat was at the front –

enormous, with an even back and a head like a slab. Stana frothed at the mouth and cursed him. Her glasses gave off angry sparks. The goat gifted her with a slow violet gaze and continued on his way. The she-goats trotted after him.

Stana looked out for her Bucha, but she wasn't there. After the last goat had gone by, Stana stood as if struck by lightning. Bucha was all she had in this world. Her little Bucha, her stupid, darling Bucha. Stana's hackles went up and this time, she remained at her gate to face the goatherd, ready to scratch his eyes out if necessary.

At last, here he was – limping along in a whirlwind of dust, and brick-red in the face. The closer he came, the more Stana worked herself up. Then she saw Bucha next to him. And in his hands he was holding something.

'There,' the goatherd stepped towards her and handed it over, 'It's yours. A male.'

Stana was holding a downy creature with long legs, tiny hooves gleaming like pearls and beautiful eyes. Bucha stretched her neck and licked her baby. It gave out a feeble bleat.

When Stana looked up, Zlatko's broad back was once again engulfed by a cloud of dust. She could hear only the pebbles and dry twigs that broke under his limp foot as he went downhill.

Stana stood like this for a while, the baby goat in her arms, then she took it inside the house. She darted about until she'd found a box of matches. She came to the rubbish dump and lit it in several places. The fire took instantly and soared, lighting up the village and the sky above it. All night, its hellish black smoke drew a path up to the moon.

The next day, Stana was at her little gate earlier than usual. The dump was gone. The dewdrops on the roof of the house looked like emeralds fallen from the heavens overnight. When the goatherd approached, Stana gave Bucha a timid push.

Around Bucha's neck was the necklace of red beads.

A Nocturne for Ventsi

HE COULDN'T GET A GRIP ON HIS MEMORY. IT WAS YET ANOTHER weakness on top of all his other pathetic weaknesses. Again and again, pictures from their marriage emerged in his mind, fragments of conversations, all their break-ups, and in between either sun-struck meadows, or the black abyss of not knowing. Black and full of crows.

He decided that he had to get away and keep moving. He packed a sports bag and set off. But nothing could save him from his memories – not the early mornings at railway stations, not arrivals in small towns at sunset, nor the sweet sadness of absinth, nor the broad fields where deer grazed. His memories kept coming back at him, finding new ways to devastate him.

Ventsi kept walking – small and lonely, and full of questions. He didn't know that his questions had no answer, because all answers about love immediately turn into new questions.

In a small provincial town he bought a toy gun. He started drawing bulls' eyes everywhere – in the dusty sides of the road, in the plaster of houses at the end of village streets. He imagined them on the faces of unpleasant people he knew. Then he would take out the gun and fire. And for a moment, he almost felt better.

'So what if I'm short,' he said to himself. 'So what if I'm quiet from time to time. So what if I can't dance. And I don't know boxers, pop singers, barmen, writers and show hosts. So what? I gave her a home and a family, didn't I? Didn't she say that she wanted us to get married?'

On he went, putting one foot in front of the other in the roadside dust, and asking questions. If he stopped, his evil memory would flood him again right where he stood, on a little island of oblivion. And behind him he would hear the crows drawing closer.

'So what if she's popular. They come looking for her, they take her out to posh restaurants and talk about Freud. She had to choose *someone*. She said she liked it with me. I gave her a home and a family.'

Then he sat down in the roadside dust and drew bulls' eyes. And he fired at them with his toy gun. But there was no sound.

A lorry gave him a lift to the waterfall. He continued uphill on foot, along the narrow mountain road.

'Hi there, boy.'

'Hello,' he said to the old man. Except he wasn't an old man at all. His hair was thick and bristly like bear's fur. He carried a sack full of something on his back, but didn't seem to find it heavy.

'Acorns,' he explained. 'Acorns for the pigs. Where are you going?'

What could Ventsi say – I'm running away from the crows?

'Up the hill,' he said.

The man looked at the sky, at the pine forest. His rubber galoshes were smeared with mud.

'You're not gonna make it tonight. Better come home with me. Stay the night, and tomorrow, God willing… I'm Trenko.'

At home, his wife offered them goat's cheese and tomatoes. Then she returned to her chair and picked up her knitting.

'What brings you this way, boy?' she asked.

What could Ventsi say?

'I'm looking for an edelweiss flower,' he said quietly. Trenko's wife twitched, startled. Her hair was tied up in a tight headscarf.

'Do you want to hear a tale?' she said, and without waiting for his answer, she was off. Her words ran smooth like beautiful, dense knitwork.

'The king decided to marry his daughter off, and grooms-to-be came from all over the kingdom. Princes, dukes, all manner of noblemen and heroes. There was in his kingdom a young swineherd. He was herding his swine one day, when the bear

44

came and said: "Little swineherd, give me a piglet and I'll tell you what the king's daughter has on her knees." The swineherd gave the bear a piglet and she told him that the king's daughter had stars on her knees. In a while, the bear came back and said: "Little swineherd, give me another piglet and I'll tell you what the king's daughter has on her bellybutton." The boy gave her another piglet and the bear said: a moon. When the bear came again and got another piglet, she told him the king's daughter had a sun on her breast. And the swineherd lost his sleep. One day, his mother baked him a loaf of bread, gave him a bunch of sweet-smelling flowers from the garden, crossed herself and let him go. He went to the king's court. The king sits there and asks the grooms-to-be: what does the king's daughter have on her knees? And they all sit there dumb, but the swineherd goes, "Stars." And on her bellybutton? Moon. And on her breast? Sun. And the king gave him his daughter.'

The woman had stopped knitting. Her eyes fixed him darkly. Trenko had fallen asleep with his hat on. Suddenly, the woman jumped up off her chair, gathered her skirts and pulled the rough woollen sock down. She tore off her headscarf. Her hair spilled out and shone in the dark like pure gold.

'Here, take a good look. Stars, moon, sun. All nonsense, you say!'

And Ventsi saw that over each knee, on the lily-white, unnaturally young skin, there was a star.

In the morning, Ventsi took off early. Fog crept up the hillsides. The pine trees swished high over his head, enormous and unreal. The last thing he heard was the joyful grunting of the pigs while Trenko and his wife fed them.

Around the corner, Ventsi stopped. The sun boomed high up in the pines. He took out his gun and put it in his mouth. But there was no sound.

Maria

WHILE SHE SAT ON A PARK BENCH AND FED THE PIGEONS
with croissants, Maria suddenly realised that the man sitting
over there on that bench had a dreadful headache. He had his
hands over his face. She smiled and sent him a ray, then a few
more. The pigeons took off at once, as if they'd been shot, then
landed on the branches of a nearby tree and fixed Maria with
their orange eyes. In a few minutes, the man on the bench let go
of his face and looked around him. Then he took off down the
alley at a lively pace. Maria made herself more comfortable on
her bench and continued to crumble a croissant.

A boy and a girl sat on the bench opposite. The girl was looking straight ahead, her face stony. The boy was saying something
animatedly, his arms waving, his voice rising until he burst into
tears. Maria knew that the girl was late for a rendezvous and

couldn't give a toss about the boy. Maria smiled and sent a very strong ray in the direction of the girl. The pigeons took off again. The girl shivered, looked at the weeping boy and slowly slipped her hand under his t-shirt and stroked his back. He couldn't believe it. The girl licked his nose and kissed him so passionately that the world around them went silent.

After those two were gone, the bench remained empty. The pigeons finished off the crumbs and flew away. The sky was darkening in the south. The sudden wind swept the rubbish along the alley. Crushed plastic cups trotted along like horses. Spectacular lightning in the form of a Chinese hieroglyph flashed in a blink, then the heavens opened. Maria relaxed on her bench and surrendered to the rain.

Late in the afternoon, a mother with a small boy walked along the empty alley. The boy was kicking about, scattering the wet autumn leaves and splashing in the puddles when his mother wasn't looking. He stopped by the bench where Maria had sat.

'Look, Mum,' he said and touched the wet bench wood. 'Maria was sitting here.'

'Who is this Maria?' his mother asked. The boy ran along.

'Bobby, who is this Maria you were talking about?' she said when she caught up with him.

But Bobby kept quiet. He had suddenly realised that he couldn't explain to his mother about Maria.

The Big Green Locust

I RAN INTO THEIR LITTLE EXPEDITION IN THE HAYMAKING season. A boy with long, shiny chestnut hair and big luminous eyes led the way. In his right hand he held a stub with a faded flag on top. I'd been drinking and wanted company. I went along with them. The kids took no notice of me. They kept walking with great concentration. Their dusty feet were wrapped in rags and made light, rhythmic tapping noises along the road.

'So where are you off to?' I asked the boy at the front. I could pass as their older comrade, surely. The boy ignored me and kept his eyes on the road. I lagged behind and walked with the others further back. A red-haired girl winked at me. It sent shivers down my spine. It wasn't at all a childish wink, oh no.

'You little bitch, why are you winking at me?' I growled quietly. Look at them. Off their own bat, waving some stupid flag, and on top of that they wouldn't talk to me.

In the evening, we stopped by some abandoned sheep-pens. I noticed that the group was highly organised. A few boys rushed off to bring wood for burning, others piled up some stones and they stoked an excellent fire. The girls dashed off to the nearby fields and came back with potatoes tied up in their tracksuit tops.

Night fell quickly. The crickets started screeching and their tiny violins sparkled in the grass blades like dew. The children ate fire-baked potatoes in silence, drank water from a giant, velvet-soft gourd and went off to catch fireflies which they stuck on their foreheads. The leader with the big luminous eyes stayed by the fire. I approached and slumped down heavily next to him. My mouth was dry. I pulled out the rakia bottle from my ruck-sack and took a great big gulp.

'So,' I said. 'Is there anything you want to tell me?'

'Why do you torment yourself, señor?' the boy said gently. 'Why do you want to know everything? Just walk with us if you find it pleasant. You might walk for a couple of days and get bored, and give up.'

'Listen,' I said. 'I've lost a whole day walking with you. I think you need to explain what's going on.'

'The explanation is up to you, señor. Look at the fire, keep quiet and it might come to you. It will land on your conscious-ness like a big green locust.'

'You know what, you little shit? I could be your father. Explain yourself to me, damn it.'

The boy didn't reply. His eyes had a pensive look. In each of them, a little fire burned. At this point, the red-haired girl came flying out of the darkness. She smiled at me, smacked my face with her pony-tail and before I knew it, she'd slapped something on my forehead. Then she disappeared again into the dark.

'You're a very sad man, señor,' the boy said. 'You have a homeless look. Your beard has started going grey. Your breathing is hard. You drink, although you know that with each gulp of rakia the well of sadness only goes deeper. You're trying to threaten me, but you're not up to it. Have a good sleep tonight. The big green locust is already flexing his mighty back legs. Ready to jump. You have to go and greet him.'

The boy turned away, lay on the warm earth and fell asleep. The other kids were also settling down for the night inside the empty pens. I breathed in the night for a while, contemplated the fire, then put a little dry stump under my head and drifted off.

Birdsong woke me up. When I opened my eyes, I couldn't believe the clarity and the brightness of the day. The atmosphere hummed with purity and sunshine. Little transparent angels seemed to float in the air. The ashes of the fire still gave off heat. Nearby, I saw a neat human column, all ready to go. They were patiently waiting for me. I reached for my shoes, but they

51

suddenly seemed horribly oversized, heavy and crude, so I ditched them and ran off in my bare feet to join the column.

I found myself right next to my red-haired acquaintance. She whipped her pony-tail across my face again, and off we went. Then she nudged me and gave me something in her closed fist. I took it carefully in my palm, closed my fingers and looked inside. There, with his wings at rest, and flexing his mighty back legs, was a big green locust. I felt the confident pulsing of his body inside my fist. I smiled to myself and opened my hand. The locust flew out far ahead like an arrow shot from a bow.

'What's your name?' I asked the red-haired girl as we walked on. Her intelligent, happy eyes darted at me, and she opened her mouth. It took me a while to work out what she was trying to show me, then I saw it. Her tongue had been cut out.

I looked in desperation to the leader. His heavy chestnut hair was swinging between his shoulder blades. Then he turned around as if I'd called him. His big luminous eyes looked at me encouragingly.

Koko

In memory of Yordan Radichkov

THE SWINE WAS DUE TO GIVE BIRTH DAYS AGO BUT DIDN'T.
She just lay on the hay, bulky as a mountain, and groaned from
time to time. Alec went in a few times to check up on her, even
late at night with a flickering torch. But the swine's frightful head
rested lifelessly in the wet hay, and all Alec saw was a sad starlet
of an eye. Perhaps it wasn't even that.

The following day, they fussed about and waited. In the mid-
afternoon, Alec's grandfather put his cap on and went to get the
vet. Alec remembered the vet from back when he'd brought his
male pig round. It was a small but terrifyingly powerful beast
with a long black snout. Before they put him in the sty with
the swine, they'd sent Alec away so he wouldn't watch. Alec
pretended to go, but he went round the back and found a brok-
en brick, and he saw it all through the crack. The swine trotted

in a circle for a while, but the male eventually caught up with her and mounted her. While the hellish beast was riding her, the swine tipped her head up to the sky and a sad fog fell over her eyes.

The vet arrived in his clapped-out horse cart, small as a walnut shell, and jumped off heavily. The earth trembled with his hundred and fifty kilos. Alec looked with fascination at his mighty buttocks as they ran to the sty. The vet patted the swine on the back, gave her an injection, poured down his throat the rakia Alec's grandfather brought him in a tiny glass, charged them ten lev and climbed back inside his horse cart. He whipped the massive mule, and disappeared in a cloud of soot at the end of the street.

But by the evening, nothing had changed. Alec suggested they take turns standing by the swine, but his grandfather decided that whatever was going to happen, it wouldn't happen before tomorrow, and he told Alec to go to bed. Alec woke up in the night at the sound of a drawn-out moan. His grandfather bounced out of bed. They grabbed the gas torch and rushed to the sty, but it was all over. The swine was on her side, gurgling. In the hay underneath her lay the tiny crushed bodies of five piglets. Alec's grandfather cursed, kneeled by the swine and stroked her forehead. Suddenly, she stretched her body, her eyes opened wide, her legs gave a few kicks and she died.

'Grandad, look!' Alec cried. At the swine's back feet, deep in the hay, another piglet lay whining. It was the size of Alec's palm. He grabbed it and took it to the house. He found a cardboard box, lined it with newspaper and put the piglet inside. Its legs were thinner than Alec's fingers. Its eyes were still glued together and its minuscule hooves were soft and pink, but the funniest thing was its tail – it looked like spaghetti. Alec found a syringe and squirted a little milk in the piglet's mouth. It went to sleep.

His grandfather took one look at the creature, washed his hands and muttered before going to bed: 'You won't make a man out of this.'

The next day, the piglet was doing better. It wasn't trembling any more, it was gripping the syringe with its mouth and even trying to get up. Alec fed it every three hours, and the rest of the time it slept. Alec called it Koko.

The end of summer was drawing near. The mornings came suddenly, like thunder, but a star shone in the sky for a long time after. Early in the morning, Alec and Koko went walking in the garden. Alec would lag behind and lay down on his belly in the cool dew. Koko looked for him. He'd rush this way and that, sniffing the earth, or freeze and look around in panic. His tiny ears throbbed together with his heart. A falling leaf was enough to startle him, and he'd take off in a random direction. He was stronger now, and reached up to Alec's ankle. In the end Koko would always find Alec among the clumps of earth. He looked like a tiny pink locomotive as he flew towards Alec. He'd stop by

Alec's nose and look at him crossly. But soon his anger would pass and he'd start kissing Alec with his soft snout – his nose, his hair, his hands. His soft grunting gave away his happiness.

Koko was a bit of a pain, actually. He wouldn't leave Alec's side, except to get into trouble. According to his mood, flashes of colour would pass over his forehead. His long white lashes made him look like a seasoned hooligan. But his hooves remained his best feature: shiny and polished like tiny porcelain shoes.

'Koko!' Alec would call, and Koko would arrive in a wild trot from the world's end, his snout covered in pear juice, his hooves smeared in golden goo, and he'd rub himself against Alec's leg as if to apologise for stuffing his face illicitly with the fallen pears. And he'd nudge Alec, his way of asking to go for a walk together. Still Alec wouldn't move. He was waiting for Koko to perform his pièce de résistance. Koko clocked it instantly – he'd go and take Alec's sandal in his mouth, and bring it to him in a wild rush. Then the other sandal. And then he'd look at Alex with his cherry eyes. Now, he was saying, you can't get out of it. So Alec would put on his sandals and off they'd go to explore the big wide world.

They liked to go and inspect the allotment, for example. In the blossoms of thistle, drugged bees were sleeping. In the distance, they'd spot a donkey, standing there like an ancient monument to philosophy. The jagged outline of the forest drew nearer. In the sunny spots the world's best berries grew, and Alec and Koko gorged on them until they were sick. On the side of the bog lay big fat black oxen, like devils. Some of them would rise at the sight of Alec and Koko, their horns touching the declining sun. Alec and Koko took off and ran for dear life – across the thorns, across the berry bushes, across the flocks of geese which crowed and covered the world in down – and they only stopped running when they reached home, weak with sun and hunger.

Mid-September was approaching. It was time to think about school again. Alec liked to think how he'd take Koko with him to Sofia. But he shook the thought away each time. After all, they were both real men, and had to find the strength to say goodbye.

'I'll be back soon,' Alec told his piglet as he held Koko on his knees and looked straight into his eyes. 'One morning, you'll get up and you'll see that everything around you is white with snow, and then you can get out on the road and wait for me. You won't have to wait more than an hour or two, then I'll be there, coming round the bend, and you'll rush to me and we'll be the best of bros in the world. You just wait for me, Koko.'

Koko caught Alec's breath with his sensitive nostrils, and his forehead furrowed with effort.

His grandfather saw him off to the bus. They'd shut Koko in the sty, to stop him chasing after Alec. But Koko saw Alec's departure through a crack in the sty, and he started squealing so desperately that Alec had to turn his heart into stone to stop himself from going back.

His time in Sofia was eventful. In the autumn, Alec shaved for the first time, observing with great excitement the few black hairs that grew on his face. He also started getting calls from a girl, and together they covered miles of city pavement, kicking the autumn leaves and kissing. The girl had glasses, and before they kissed, she'd carefully remove them and put them in a little velvet case.

Then it was the winter holidays and his mother tactfully reminded him that he'd promised to drop in and see his grandfather. It took him by surprise – he'd made other plans already. But he didn't want to break his promise, so he put on his winter boots, and with the grim face of a weather-beaten traveller, he set off in the snow for the railway station. On the train, he met an escaped prisoner and they drank beer together. The prisoner knew he'd be caught at the next station, so he was going to jump off the train – but he kept putting it off. Finally, he finished his beer and looked at Alec.

'Don't look if you don't want to,' he said. Then he went to the carriage's exit door, opened it and stood before the thundering hole for a while. Outside, there was a black whirlwind, smoke and mountains, and unearthly beams pierced the night. It looked as if some mighty engine was spinning the world outside the carriage door.

"Bye!' the prisoner cried, and jumped.

Alec arrived in the village late at night. His grandfather was overjoyed to see him. He fried sixteen eggs for him, poured him a glass of wine and afterwards, heavy with food and travel, Alec slept like a stone.

He woke up around midday. Through the frosty window, he saw a red light outside. He wondered, annoyed, what was happening. He got up, washed his hands and went outside. In the middle of the yard, in a shallow hole, there was a bed of hot embers. Three stubbly men in rough sweaters were warming their hands over them. Alec's grandfather held a tray with four small yellow glasses.

'Cheers,' he said. 'May it go well.' The men delicately picked up the little glasses and tossed the contents straight into their throats.

'You want some?' his grandfather asked Alec. Alec nodded. His grandfather poured him a little glass and Alec, imitating the men, drank it all at once. After the rakia, things started moving and time sped up a bit.

'The boy can help too,' one of the men said. He had startling pale blue eyes, like a Hollywood actor. He opened the door of the sty. The hog stepped out heavily on stiff legs. Shouting and shoving, the men drove him to the bed of fire.

'Let's go,' said the blue-eyed man. The three pushed down on the animal until it keeled. The blue-eyed man drew a thin knife from his leather belt and deftly inserted it into the hog's throat. The animal gave a snort and kicked. In two minutes, it was all over.

'Clean work,' said the blue-eyed man.

Late in the afternoon, the feast was ready. The butchers sat around the table in the biggest room. The coal stove was red-hot. Alec was strangely excited. His grandfather brought a new bottle of rakia and took a tray of pork ribs from the stove, sprinkled with parsley.

It was delicious, and they stuffed their faces. After two big plates of ribs, Alec drank more rakia and his mind became even foggier. I've overdone it, he thought. He got up and went outside to get some fresh air. The yard was white like a fairy tale, with a faint red glow in the middle. At least twenty cats had come to scatter the entrails and lick the bloody snow. Alec took two more steps, and it suddenly hit him.

In the cement open-air sink, in a big tray, lay the severed head of the hog. Alec touched it. This head had nothing in common with Koko.

Alec washed his hands in the sink and went into the sty. On the frozen ground, there were a few clumps of blackened hay. The cement trough had been washed clean.

Alec turned this way and that, and was about to leave when his foot caught on something. He foraged in the hay and picked it up. It was his two sandals, stuck together and solid like iron. He tried to prise them apart, but they were stuck for good.

The General

I DID MY ARMY SERVICE IN THE TOWN OF N., THE SECOND largest in Bulgaria. Our squad had its own park and vegetable garden, an exemplary pig sty, beautifully painted watchtowers and an embankment that rose high on one side of the estate. Over the embankment the sun disappeared every day, except sometimes it would linger. It was over the embankment that the wind sometimes brought us the sound of women's steps. And it was in the embankment that we were always digging our trenches, and there, in its hard clay slopes, we buried our empty bottles. As you might have guessed, such an estate could only be governed by a general. And so it was.

I was under his personal command. I had the honour of accompanying him on his morning runs. The general ran at a hundred miles per hour. His silk tracksuit flapped in the wind.

The general kept his speed up. Before the finale, he would turn into a red flash. I tried not to lag too far behind. Towards the end, you could practically feel the earth spin. And right at the end of our run, not a minute too early or too late, the sun rose – and like a gong it announced the start of the day.

The next activity was shaving. The general would take a shower, and his body gave off a white vapour in the cold air. The barber, a provincial guy from a long line of barbers that trailed off into past centuries, had to take extra care. He would dive in and out of the general's body vapour. This guy was so good, he was the Paganini of barbers. We all stood by, to attention. We waited for the vapour to disperse and for the diamond-smooth face of the general to emerge from it. He was a real general, you see, so he never did things by halves.

'Are we all set, boys?' We'd hear his voice and visibly relax. When the general spoke, it was a signal that all was well. My mate Pancho even allowed himself to stand on one leg like a stork, to rest his other leg, he said.

'So, we crack on today,' the general said. 'Every day is the beginning of something. Every beginning is difficult. But for those with a clear purpose, the day is a joy.'

A lieutenant would open his ring binder and unclip the schedule for today, the twentysomething of the year nineteen something-or-other. It was all written in wondrous colours, the words perched along their lines like hummingbirds.

'Today,' the general read out, 'the fish to be put in the pool. Where's the commanding officer of the Rear Unit?'

Shivers ran through Pancho, me and the two colonels. Only we knew that there was still no water in the pool.

'Sorry,' the general said, 'that's for tomorrow. Today, the pool to be filled with water. Where's the CO of the Rear Unit?'

It was like a breeze passing through birch trees. Pancho, me, the two colonels and the lieutenants visibly relaxed.

'Evlogy!'

'Sir!'

'What's happening with the lions, Evlogy?'

'Sir!'

'What's happening with the lions? Didn't I say, two lions with big scary open maws! Small fountains are to come out of the maws and continuously flow into the pool.'

I'm Evlogy. I'd graduated in sculpture in Sofia. They said I had a bright future.

'What's happening with the lions, Evlogy?'

'Sir! You told us to go to Sofia for a week and look at lions.'

'Did you go to Sofia and look at lions, Evlogy?'

'No sir!'

The colonels were visibly shrinking. Me and Pancho were growing bigger. Pancho graduated from the Fine Art School in Tryavna, the capital of wood-carving. He could carve you a beetle so real it could fly.

'Off you go, and don't come back without inspiration.'

'Sir!'

'Sir!'

Then the rush, the crazy, heady rush across the morning dew, over the slippery stone bridge, across the big green field and the steaming clumps of earth, the taste of blood in the throat, go Pancho, go bro. Then we're on the sleepy express train from Burgas to Sofia, on the red velvet seats of the empty first-class compartments, then the ticket inspector comes with his gentle limp and blue eyes, then the first beers of the day. Yes madam, the seat's free. Where are you going? We're going to Lions' Bridge in Sofia, oh yes, we're specialists in lions, but note, madam, not just the lions of the Lions' Bridge, but also the lions in front of the Ministry of Internal Affairs, and the lions in front of the National Library too, and let's not forget the giant lions fronting the National History Museum, and it goes without saying, the modernist lion by the eternal fire of the Unknown Soldier.

Sir! Sir! Sir!

Then it was day two, and day three. Pancho got himself a girl-friend, her name was Dewdrop. The lions in Sofia were great, they didn't budge from their places.

Back at the base, we cast our concrete lions in twenty-four hours. The entire Third Home Company was mobilised to help. Their senior officer was called Kiro and I called him by name. I even sent him to the kiosk on an errand at one point. By sunrise, our two lions were open-mawed and terrifying, their tails practically twitching. After his shave, the general came to see them. He liked it that their maws were so big and scary. And just as the lieutenant with the ring binder was handing him the day's schedule, the general froze. We all froze with him.

'Sir!'

'Sir!'

'Why is this lion without a mane?'

It was without a mane because Pancho and I accidentally broke the plaster cast moments before we were about to cast the second lion in concrete. But otherwise, they were both equally open-mawed, equally terrifying.

'It's a lioness, Comrade General, sir!' Pancho chimed brightly.

'Lioness? How come?'

'A lion and a lioness, sir. That's how they are in nature. That's how they are in Sofia.'

The General straightened up. The sergeants started breathing again.

'Attention, Evlogy! Attention, Pancho! Well done!'

'Sir! Sir! We serve the People's Republic, sir!'

Then the hummingbirds stirred on their branches.

'Right. Today, the twentysomething of the something… Water to flow from the open maws of the lions. Where's the CO of the Rear Unit? Where are the fish?'

The fish were goners. The fish were long swimming in the river Styx. The entire personnel were breathing heavily, their mouths open with terror.

'The pumps aren't working, Comrade General, sir!'

'What is working, then?'

'The brook at the upper end of the estate.'

'Form a chain. Find buckets. Start now!'

The lieutenants cast off their tunics. Their white bodies shone like moons next to the dark bodies of the squaddies. The colonels undid their top three buttons.

'Bro,' Pancho said in the midst of the chaos. 'We've got to fix the lioness tonight. She's got balls. Remember, you worked like a dog to make them look good. We've got to break them off tonight.'

'Pancho! Evlogy!'

Up in the blue sky a lark was singing. It must have been the haymaking season. It must have been summer – the summer of nineteen something-or-other.

'Sir!'

'Sir!'

'You two. Begin the horse. It's a no-brainer. He stands on his four legs, rock solid. Like the lions. Like in nature. No neighing, no nonsense. He's looking straight ahead, in a bright and cheer-ful manner. Scale, three to one.'

That night, after Pancho and I fixed the lioness, we had a

smoke. We lay listening to the crickets, and fell asleep with our eyes open.

The idea to make the horse hollow came to both of us simultaneously. Not because we'd read the *Iliad* that carefully – it was just that otherwise it would drag on, and we'd never get discharged. Even so, the horse took us ages. First, the cast broke. Then the concrete poured out and made the horse look like he was wading in fresh lava. The CO of the Rear Unit brought an electric chainsaw, mighty like a wild boar. We scraped the lava away, we practically licked it off. There was just a day and a half left before our discharge. The horse was standing on his four legs, rock solid. Pancho got wasted on beer and cognac. The next day he looked like one of those discarded stuffed owls you find in musty school corridors.

'We'll make it from polystyrene,' Pancho said. 'We'll put plaster on top. Then a lick of cement glue, and hey presto.'

I believed him straight away. I would believe anything at that point.

At four in the morning, we were finishing the horse under the beams of sixteen massive projectors. The Third Home Company had worked their arses off on the scaffolding that day, and now they were sleeping like they'd had their throats cut. These boys had one more year of dreamless sleep ahead of them. Sweet dreams, soldiers.

Pancho finished painting the tail with cement glue. Then he

kicked it accidentally and its end broke, so he had to make the end again. When he finally walked away, his left shoulder was twitching strangely.

I climbed up the scaffolding and stepped inside the horse. Right in the middle of his back we'd left a small opening, for the finishing touches. I walked about inside the horse. It had turned out pretty well, our horse. I sat in the spot where his heart would have been, roughly. I drifted off. I heard a faint knock, and a faint whistling. Then I must have fallen asleep.

The brass band woke me up. I jumped, hauled myself up and looked through the horse's eyes. It was pouring with rain. The personnel were all gathered in the shape of a horseshoe. A sudden gust of wind ripped off one of the horse's ribs. I grabbed it on time. 'The rain will melt it,' I thought to myself. 'Dear God, if we don't get discharged in the next hour the horse will be nothing but a puddle.'

The music stopped. Through the torrents of water, I heard the general's voice.

'Discharged from the ranks of the Bulgarian National Army after two years of service are Private Evlogy Krustev Grancharov and Private Pancho Simov Bliznakov, as of today, 4 October 1981. For exemplary service I personally award them five extra days of leave. Hurrah!'

'Hurrah!' the ranks bellowed. I gripped the rib with both hands, and for some reason, in the midst of the storm's gusts and torrents, I got the strange idea that the general was crying. I dropped the rib, jumped up and looked through the eyes of the horse again. From here, the general looked small, he looked unshaven and crumpled in his uniform, and yes – he really was crying.

Ballad for Mario

MARIA WAS ALWAYS WAITING FOR ME BEHIND THE IRON door. She sat on the black couch in the corner, broad and ample like a Madonna, looking at the blue sky. The hospital ceilings were all painted to resemble a bottomless blue sky. It was Professor K's idea. He believed that the harmonious sky-blue colour brought peace to the patients' souls. He was probably right. That's why he was a professor.

'Hello doctor,' Maria said.

I never argued with her. And anyway, I enjoyed being a doctor.

'Hi,' I said.

Maria came with me along the long shiny corridor.

'I quit smoking,' she said triumphantly. 'The cigarettes are very bad for my little baby. Right, doctor?'

And she stroked her belly tenderly. I nodded.

'That's excellent, Maria.'

In the office, the other night orderly was already waiting. We called her Auntie Velichka.

'Poor thing,' she said when she saw that Maria was hanging about in the doorway, waiting for me. 'Every two or three months, she's back. And she's always pregnant. When women lose the plot, God help us, it's always stuff like that.'

I looked out of the window – it was snowing again. Here and there, snowflakes gleamed in the night like full stops and dashes in some strange new Morse code. Muted noises came from upstairs – something was going on in the men's ward. Things could get out of hand there too, but at least they didn't have pregnancies.

Auntie Velichka and I finished drinking our tea and went about doing our job. In the canteen, I found Maria again.

'Doctor,' she said, 'I've decided to call my baby Mario. But don't tell anyone, it's a secret. I have this incredible presentiment that it's a boy. Look at these pigment marks on my face.'

I assured her that the pigment marks were fine. It was midnight before I managed to get back to the office and open one of my textbooks.

Suddenly, there was an urgent banging on the door.

'Come and see what she's up to.' It was Auntie Velichka. She rushed off again.

In room number six, all the lights were on. The other women were sitting on their beds, watching Maria with distress. I went straight over. Maria's bed sheets and clothes were on the floor. She lay on the mattress stark naked, bathed in sweat, her arms tucked behind her back and clutching one another. At regular intervals, Maria strained horribly and gave out a scream. Her eyes were ready to pop out.

'She's giving birth,' Auntie Velichka nudged me.

'Maria,' I said. 'Maria, please stop it now. You're not due yet.'

When she heard my voice, Maria calmed down.

'Doctor, you'll tell me when it's time, won't you?'

'You can be sure of that, Maria. That's what I'm here for.'

She put on her clothes and went to bed.

I woke up at around four in the morning and decided to do a check-up tour of the ward. When I opened the door of the bathroom, I froze. Sitting on the window sill was a woman. The window was open and snowflakes drifted through the iron bars and landed in her hair. It was Maria.

'Maria,' I called out quietly, so as not to startle her, 'you'll catch cold like this.'

She looked up from her folded knees.

'You know, my baby will be called Mario. An excellent name, isn't it, doctor? Do you know, he's getting used to his name. When I say Mario, he gives a little kick. Tap-tap. Tap-tap.'

I sat on the wooden bench and lit a cigarette. Maria came

down from the sill and crouched beside me. Her shadow grew enormous for a moment, then seemed to throw itself onto the wet floor, face down. I looked at Maria's broad face, her trembling eyelids. She looked at me, too. Whenever I looked into the eyes of our female patients, I had the same feeling. It was like trying to read a book by looking at the text reflected in a mirror. You don't understand a thing, but you know there's something written there.

'Doctor, let's get married,' Maria begged quietly. 'Nobody will know. I want my baby to have a daddy.'

The snow kept drifting in through the open window. Maria got up and took my hand. She signed her name on the damp tiles of the wall, then I signed mine. She was serious and formal. The water pipes gurgled some sad and wonderful music. We stood like this for a while, then Maria reached inside her pocket and retrieved two rings made from foil. She pushed one down my finger, and put the other one on. A little spider ran across the ceiling. Maria's hands were icy cold. With chattering teeth, she started unbuttoning her pyjamas.

'Maria,' I said. 'Let's put you to bed.'

Maria stood there with her freckled shoulders slumped, then put her pyjamas back on and obediently started walking to room number six. I fiddled with the foil ring for a while and then tossed it in the bin.

In the morning, after my shift, Auntie Velichka sent me off

73

with a hot tea. My head felt numb with sleeplessness as I walked home. For the first time in months, the winter sky was broken up, and in the cracks a wild blue chill gleamed at us. In the bright air, people's faces shone like new coins. I went into the first open pastry shop I saw and slumped at a table. At the next table were a father and son. I was minding my own business, drinking my coffee, when I saw that the boy was staring at me intently. I had no idea why I'd attracted the attention of a ten-year-old boy. His face was beautiful and judgemental. His eyes were made from wonderful velvet. Damn it, I thought, aren't you going to leave soon? He was making me uncomfortable. But his big dark eyes wouldn't let go of me.

The father finished his pastry, wiped his mouth with his palm and got up.

'Come on, Mario,' he said.

The boy rose from his chair and took his father by the hand. But even after they went out into the street, even through the shop window, his luminous eyes were still on me. They were full of hatred.

Queen Bee

EVERY NIGHT, MY WIFE AND I LAY NEXT TO EACH OTHER IN bed and stared into the darkness with wide-open eyes. Come closer, I begged her, but she would place her narrow hand on my chest and say: We mustn't. You know we mustn't. Even though it was dark as hell, I could see the desire in her eyes, but I could also see the fear which was a thousandfold stronger than the desire. No one will know, I whispered hoarsely, and she kept quiet until I'd start kissing the plaster on the wall. Then she'd say, You don't know them, they know everything, they find out everything sooner or later.

In the end, we'd fall asleep. My wife twitched in her sleep like a sea-horse, and I longed for her honey-coloured skin, her beautiful eyes, her red hair which I so loved to stroke once upon a time; I longed for her smooth limbs. Then the flood of sleep engulfed me.

In the morning, we'd pretend nothing had happened. We'd have a silent cup of coffee and part, secretly touching with our eyelashes. When she was leaving, I'd yell: 'It's your turn today to see him!' and despite the distance between us, I sensed her gratitude. We were supposed to take turns, but I always gave up my turn. Her visit to the child was her day's highlight. I'd been to the children's home a few times, of course, but our little boy had long forgotten me. He would dutifully sit next to me on the bench and wait for our visit to be over. A gong announced the end of the visit. A tall woman with a golden-black apron would get the children to stand in rows, and off they would go, singing a song all the way back across the vast, perfectly mowed lawn. I would rather my wife went to these visits, and then tell me about it: about every word our little boy had said, every movement, every little hair on his head. Her accounts were so lovely that they created another world for me, a world I needed more than I needed real memories.

At night, before going to bed, we watched TV. The programme lasted from eight till ten. There were often reports from children's homes or boarding schools, and we gazed avidly at all the kids. At ten o'clock the power went off and we went to bed. I bit my hands and tried not to speak, but eventually I'd beg her all over again: Please, come closer. My wife would touch my chest with her palm again and say: We mustn't. I'd turn to the wall and kiss its coarse surface, and torrents of water kept collapsing inside my head.

The arrival of the first bees went unnoticed. We only saw them when they had covered the window sill. Then they went away, and we'd almost forgotten about it, when suddenly they returned in greater numbers. They sat in big clusters along the sill, they darkened the windows and they stayed there all day in big, golden clumps. At dusk, I went out for a walk. Walking in pairs was forbidden. Along the way, I saw solitary men and women who were trying to look happy. I too made sure to flash a smile from time to time. It was the prudent thing to do. When I came home, the flat was packed full of bees. They covered the walls and the ceiling, and their terrible buzzing made my hair stand on end. My wife lay in bed, covered from head to toe with a solid sheet of bees. I stared at her with speechless horror. Suddenly, as if by command, the bees took off and I saw that her body was bound up in black and gold ribbons. Her hair was pulled violently up away from her forehead, and her beautiful eyes had a squint. I didn't even know if she could see me. Suddenly, she said: 'You'll have to go now, my darling. They will start stinging you very soon. I asked them not to kill you and they gave me their promise. Don't waste time. Goodbye, my darling. It was good being with you.'

'What's happening?' I asked, then the air lurched and I felt the first stings. 'Go,' she said. She had difficulty speaking now. 'Don't ask questions.' I tried to steady myself against the wall, but my hand sank into a sticky golden-black goo and at once became enormous. I pushed the door open and stumbled outside. I was losing my wits. My swollen lips couldn't make any sound. I could hardly see. Blood poured from my temples. The bees pursued me for a while, then left me alone. I sat on the stone pavement. I was grateful to the bees for one thing: their complete, utter honesty.

The Mute

I'D BEEN LOOKING FOR THE WATER SPRING ALL DAY, WITH no joy. The sun was setting and it was time to turn back. The old woman and the boy appeared out of nowhere. They must have climbed up to the road using a steep, narrow path in the ferns. The woman sat on a whitewashed milestone and pulled the headscarf away from her face to cool it down in the breeze. Her face was ashen with exhaustion. She started talking as if we were old acquaintances. Meanwhile, the boy squatted down and started examining close-up a column of ants that snaked along the road. He was a well-built boy and wore an old tracksuit. His eyes had an unusual brightness about them.

'We're going to the monastery,' she said. 'You know the monastery? There's no end to our plight, no end. We've done the rounds of all the churches, all the monasteries – nothing. I don't know if there's anybody up there no more. See, he's mute.' She nodded at the boy. 'He's a good boy, he understands everything, he taught himself to read, but he can't speak. Look at him, almost a lad and he can't speak…' A car passed us and we were engulfed in dust. When the dust settled, the old woman's face looked stony. The wrinkles carved her face all the way down to her bitter mouth.

'So we heard that Saint Ivan helped the dumb. They said, leave some of the boy's clothes next to his relics for a night. Then he puts on the clothes for three days. I've got the clothes and everything…'

She started rummaging in her bag, must have been for the hundredth time that day, to check she had everything.

'Some woman, Petkana's her name, started speaking after she did that,' she went on, her faded eyes fixing on the mountain slopes. 'She was seventy already, dumb since childhood. So she came to the monastery and visited Saint Ivan's cave too, and by the time she boarded the train to go home she was speaking. Some man from Dupnitsa too, he'd had an illness as a child and been dumb since then. They brought his shirt and left it at the saint's coffin. When he put it on, it was all fine again and he started speaking. And before the monastery they say there's a spring. The water gushed out way back, when the saint's relics were carried here. The procession stopped to rest and this water gushed out. Since then, they say it cures people. Somewhere

here, they said, one kilometre before the monastery. We went round but couldn't find it. They say it's very small.'

The boy had gone off the road. I saw him on the path below the road. He was opening the ferns with his hands and forging ahead. Then I lost him from view.

'I got this prayer for Saint Ivan, see. Our priest gave me it.' The woman rummaged in her bag again and pulled out a folded piece of paper almost torn along the creases. The prayer was written with an indelible pencil: 'Saint Ivan, pray to our gentle Lord Jesus Christ for our souls…'

I handed back the piece of paper.

'Take it,' she said. 'I know it by heart now. You take it.' Then she wiped her dry eyes and said: 'The boy's got faith, all right. We've got this icon of Saint Ivan at home, and he sits there and moves his lips. Sometimes, he glows like all the angels of heaven are visiting him. But to be honest with you, I don't know no more, is there someone up there, or isn't there? God forgive me for saying it,' and she quickly crossed herself. 'We've done the rounds of all the churches, all the monasteries. And nothing.'

She got up. 'We better get going. They'll close the monastery. Yovcho, come on sweetheart,' she called out and looked around. 'Where is that boy, he was here just a minute ago.'

When we stood at the end of the road, we saw him. He had crossed the small valley below the road and was kneeling on the other side, at the foot of the mountain slope. Giant fir trees rose around him. At one point, he turned around and saw us. He jumped to his feet and waved his arms at us. When we approached, I saw that his throat was swollen and his arteries were ready to burst. And suddenly, he cried out: 'Graaan!'

He had found the spring. His grandmother started shaking uncontrollably. She poured some water for him, gave him some to drink, washed his face and they were off to the monastery. The boy kept calling as they went: 'Graaan! Graaan!'

And he kept laughing and touching his wet hair.

When they disappeared from view around the bend, I kneeled before the limpid water collected in the small stone basin, its rim surrounded by bunches of geraniums, fabric threads and a tiny paper icon of Saint Ivan glued above the water spout, and I filled my cupped hands with the icy-cold water and washed my face. Then I bent down and started drinking. The spring was the same as it had been in 1964, when I used to come here with my grandmother. Exactly the same.

I drank, crunched with my teeth the sand grains in the tasty water, and cried. We had found the spring straight away back then. In the violet twilight, the monastery bells called for vespers.

The Return of the Prodigal Son

THE ALLEY THAT LED UP TO THE HOSPITAL WAS LINED WITH linden trees. I had difficulty finding my mother's room. I suggested we go outside for ten minutes. We walked a long time down the corridor, and the slippers flapped against her heels like the crack of whips. We sat on a bench. A bit of colour came into her face. Because she had difficulty talking, she preferred to be quiet and just look me in the eyes. Her pupils were like two very long tunnels. I felt tired by the end of it.

We returned the same way, down the long echoing corridor. I put my mother to bed, and she tried to smile by way of farewell. The very old woman in the other bed was looking up at the ceiling with her eyes open wide. Her white hair, fine as down, moved with the current. I closed the door quietly. Lovers were walking along the linden tree alley. Cheerful dogs trotted across the dusk. In the overflowing rubbish bins, I could hear the wasps' orgy.

I didn't feel like going home. At the tram's last stop there was an open café, so I sat in an empty chair. I didn't mind the music. The place was full of youths. The girls' legs under the tables looked like some strange vegetation. The coffee was bland, like water used to boil snails. I looked at my watch and without finishing the coffee, I went home.

I found my father in the kitchen. His hands were resting on the table like dead pigeons. In his wine glass floated tiny sails of light. I fried myself some eggs and sat in the other chair.

'Do you hear them?' my father said. I stopped chewing and pricked up my ears. The chirping really was very loud.

'I saw one today,' my father said.

'How big are they?' I asked.

'Big,' he said. 'Much bigger than we expected.'

In the corner there was a clatter, as if a whole regiment of tiny soldiers were running. I gritted my teeth and lit a cigarette. My father's face was like a big moon that kept moving in and out from behind the clouds.

'We'll have to rip up the flooring,' I said, 'and clean everything out.'

'It won't help,' my father replied. 'They live in the sewage pipes. Their kingdom is the drainage shafts. And their king is the biggest of all, with red eyes.'

84

He was drunk. I put him to sleep on the sofa bed in the kitchen. He hugged his knees and fell asleep at once. I cleaned out the ashtrays and went next door. I switched on the light, and something long and dark flipped in the corner. I overcame my disgust and went closer. There was nothing there except a chill. I lay down on the bed with my shoes on. When I woke up and looked at the clock, two hours had passed. I got up and went to look at the photos on the wall. In the cracked, lake-like surface of the images, memories and events formed overlapping concentric circles which slowly drifted somewhere. The strange ghosts on the wall filled up with blood. A warm breeze stroked my fingers.

My mother and my father as fiancés. Their hair is full of sun. My mother is wearing white socks, and my father a short-sleeved shirt. There is water behind them. My parents in some autumnal park. My mother is doe-eyed and my father is embracing her pregnant belly.

Our hospital discharge. In my parents' eyes, happiness and terror at having twins. Actually, only my brother is in the photo – I was kept in the hospital for another fifteen days after the birth, in some sort of aquarium, as they told me later. My father is younger than I am now. My mother is light like a cobweb. The bundle in my father's arms is proudly quiet. We are a few months old – naked, toothless and merry. We are crawling across a blanket full of folds, like a mountain.

We are bawling our eyes out, standing up in our little beds. The tears have formed shiny traces across our monkey faces.

My brother and I are crawling along a straw mat, staying well inside its borders. Already we are travelling in different directions. Everyone around us adores us.

My father as a young professional behind a table covered in drafts and ashtrays. His young neck is full of beautiful tendons.

My mother at some celebration in the clinic. They are handing her a banner. Her thick hair shines like a bird's wing.

Trekking in the mountains, among squirrels and pine cones.

At the seaside, photographed on top of a camel.

By the statue of Maxim Gorky, our first year at school. Our black school coats are too long and too wide, and underneath them our naked knees are scraped.

The book given to one of us (but which one is it?) has been torn, and he is crying.

A class group photo (first or second form?). Our faces are different now. My brother's beautiful Egyptian eyes are unmistakable.

A colour photo in Libya. On the cusp of puberty. We are as tall as our mother.

In Libya again. Mother with her doctor colleagues. Among them, the two-metre tall Muhammad Ali, former boxing world champion. Everyone looks at him with admiration.

Rabbit-hunting in the desert. The edges of the sand dune are finely cut, like diamonds. We didn't catch any rabbits.

Colour photo, in Varna. Our smooth golden bodies are tensed. On the alley behind us, girls in swimsuits.

Black and white photo of my brother in army uniform. The uniform ages him. His pupils don't show, he seems somehow blind, like a statue.

The surface of the photo trembled and faded. Cool air came through the open window. The small curtain blew in the current like a soul escaping a body.

Suddenly, the door lock clicked. I froze. I couldn't think who it might be. Slow steps came down the hallway. The door of my room opened and there stood my brother. We stared at each other for a while without a word. His beautiful Egyptian eyes were dead tired. His hair had gone grey. His high leather shoes gave off a strong odour.

'So you're back?' I crowed.

'Yes,' my brother said, 'till further notice.' Without moving, he quickly looked around the room in a professional manner.

'How are you doing here?' he asked.

'You know, like everyone else. It's just, the rats are a bit much…'

'I see,' my brother said, and put two fingers in his mouth and gave a piercing whistle.

In a few minutes, the room filled up with rats. They stood to attention, in thick tidy ranks, and their tails formed straight lines. Their lead eyes were fixed on my brother's. Their black bodies shivered. My brother said something incomprehensible and, screaming and squealing, the rats started jumping out of the window. When the last rat was gone, my brother rubbed his red eyes, sat on the bed and began to tell his story.

The Fall of Icarus

I NO LONGER REMEMBER JUST HOW HE CAME TO OUR HOUSE. One day I simply saw my father talking to a stranger in our courtyard. He was as tall as a tower and had no luggage. The next day, he started work in our courtyard. At the beginning, it was just a matter of digging it over, a couple of days' work. But he stayed for two weeks. He worked like an ox, twelve hours a day. He uprooted the old tree trunks left behind after the logging of the poplars. He planted a few fruit trees, and carted out the dry leaves. By the end of it, we couldn't recognise our own courtyard. He really was of another species, a species I hadn't met up till now. We called him simply the gardener.

He wasn't a piss-head, but when I poured him a glass of rakia at night, his eyes would light up. One glass, no more, my mother said, pulling me aside the first night. We can't have him getting drunk. It didn't bear imagining what it would take to reign in a drunk the size of this man. He didn't get drunk, though. He sat at the table, his enormous hands resting on top of each other like a cross. His palms were criss-crossed by a thousand lines, and looked like the estuary of the Ganges. Even from a distance, you could see this man was resting. The exhaustion of the day slowly drained away from his body. His nails were thick like tortoiseshells, and I stared at them for ages before I asked how old he was. Seventy, the man said. I was stunned. True, his face was old, rough and weathered, and his eyes were faded, but during the day I had seen his knotty chest, his taut sweaty abs shiny like copper plates, his gladiator's back and the mauve veins along his inhumanly long arms.

He was an exceptionally conscientious worker. It's as if he sifted through every handful of soil, removed the pebbles and straw, and wherever he passed, the earth became soft and smooth. After the construction of the house, the yard had been clogged with all manner of debris – broken bricks and mortar, blocks of cement, piles of wood splinters, nails, sand and quick-lime. He wiped out this lunar landscape and in its place he created a lovely garden with rye grass, pebbled paths and cypresses pointing at the sky like prayers. Here and there in the tender grass the freshly whitewashed stalks of fruit trees stuck out proudly. I never gathered the courage to ask him any more questions, for example, about where he came from, or about the big, jagged, sun-like scars on his back, covered by shiny pink skin. Even my father didn't manage to get anything more out of him, except that he came from some remote village and that in springtime he did odd jobs at people's houses.

On his last day with us, we had fine weather. The sky was as clear as a teardrop, and the air was fragrant with blossoms and shivered from time to time as golden swarms of bees darted about on their first nectar outing of the season. We had all gone outside to delight in the tender rye grass, the freshly dug trees, the pruned shrubs. That day the gardener was in particularly good spirits. From early morning he'd started making a kite for my little boy. He found the wooden boards himself, made a rhombus-shaped frame from them, stretched some coloured nylon over it and spent ages on the paper tail of the kite. My little boy was crouching beside him, completely absorbed by all this, his tongue sticking out. Only when the kite was finished did the gardener rise up in all his stature and look at me. For the first time now I saw the blueness of his eyes. They were ridiculously blue, the eyes of a child, not of a giant man with a shorn, rusty-grey head.

At lunchtime, we brought out a tablecloth and spread it over the warm earth. The gardener had a bit of food, drank his glass of rakia then sat for a while, squinting his blue eyes against the sun. Then he went off with my boy to fly the kite.

Just then, a police car pulled up in the street. Two policemen got out without rushing. The red rims of their caps cut into the afternoon silence like screeching birds.

They headed straight for the gardener. He let go of the kite and went with them obediently. It was the first time I'd seen anyone in handcuffs. They pushed him inside the car, along with the kite, then called my father and talked to him for a long time.

When the car was gone, we surrounded my father with questions, but he just stood there as if struck by lightning, his head down. Then he went inside the house, still without saying a word. My little boy was gripping me by the hand and asking, Dad, why did the policemen take him away? I had been struck dumb. Who is he, my boy kept tugging at me, what did he do? Nothing, son, I said in the end, he was a wonderful gardener, that's who he was.

Little Mister Sunshine

YURI THE POLICEMAN DRANK A CUP OF SCORCHING COFFEE
at the tin shack that grandly called itself 'Cosmos', pulled up
his collar, adjusted his gun holster at the front, and in the
falling dusk he headed towards the local park and its derelict
chapel. The chapel had been steadily decaying over the past
few years. A perpetual stench of piss hung inside and outside
its brick walls. It was a favourite haunt for all manner of low-
life.

A family had recently been robbed and beaten here. But
tonight, Yuri was going to sort out that scum. He was going to
show them who was boss. Walking along the deserted frozen
alley, he imagined kicking the chapel's door in, shining a torch
into the eyes of all those dopeheads, prostitutes and alcoholics,
lining them up along the wall and finally marching off the more

suspect-looking ones to the police station. He was sick of hearing about the chapel.

His hand on the gun holster, he reached the end of the alley and pricked up his ears. Somewhere at the other end of the park, the savage barking of a pack of countless stray dogs ripped through the night. The old willows creaked like gallows waiting for the doomed. Yuri pulled out his handgun and gripped it in his right hand, while his left hand held the torch. He kicked the door open. The inside of the chapel seemed empty. Yuri went from corner to corner, the beam of his torch searching. In one corner, he saw a small pile and went to check it out. Shards of glass crunched under his heavy army boots. Up close, the pile turned out to be a human body, lying with its face to the wall.

'Police!' Yuri bellowed, but the man didn't react. Yuri pushed him with his foot, then bent down and turned the body over. The torch shone onto the frozen corpse of an old man dressed in an ancient army coat, tied around the waist with string. The man's long beard had iced over, and was sticking straight up from his neck like a milestone. Yuri put the gun away and searched the body. In the big pockets of the coat he found a few pieces of bread, hard as iron. In the inside pocket he found something resembling a wallet, rotten and held together with an elastic band. Inside the wallet there was nothing except flecks of tobacco, and a small piece of paper containing a few words scribbled in indelible pencil. It took him a moment to decipher the writing in the torchlight.

Little Mister Sunshine, it said, I beg you…

The rest was smudged over.

The End of the War

'IT'S YOUR TURN,' BUBA SAID TO MIMI, AND POINTED AT the man in camouflage uniform at the corner table. Her shorn blond hair was cut by a shiny scar which glinted in the electric light.

'You know what, I'm sick of weirdos.' Mimi lowered her voice. 'The other day, some idiot with artificial teeth stuck a flower in my naked arse and sniffed it for an hour. In his suit and tie. I mean, he could have at least undone a button or two. Pervert. I'd rather have some drunk pig falling asleep on top of me while he's doing it. Look at this one. He looks like he just boiled his brother's ears in a big pot. I mean, I don't like men who drink and don't get drunk, they give me the creeps. You go for it if it doesn't bug you.'

'Well, they pay for it, so who cares,' Buba said.

Their establishment was open twenty-four hours and called itself 'Las Vegas', but it was just a tin shack on the side of the motorway. There were five tables inside and only grill and alcohol on the menu. The two girls waited on tables, but they also supplemented their income by taking their customers to bed. The three bungalows in the open field behind 'Las Vegas' were lovingly maintained by the girls, otherwise they would have long gone to seed.

Buba picked up a clean ashtray and headed for the man's table. She knew that after a certain number of drinks, men don't look at a woman's face, they look at her arse, and she had a good arse, everybody said so. This man checked it out too.

'Would the gentleman like anything else?' she asked.

The man opened his mouth, then gave up and just nodded at his glass. He hadn't said a word.

'Shall I keep you company?' She served him another glass of whisky. He nodded.

Buba winked triumphantly at Mimi, who was nervously observing them. Then she sat in the other chair at the man's table.

It was coming up to midnight. A lorry driver came in, his face dark with exhaustion, drank a shock dose of coffee and left. Their only customer now was the man in camouflage uniform. He stared at his glass and sipped from it at regular intervals, like a robot. From time to time, he glanced at Buba's breasts.

Then the door creaked open and Kimbo the dog sneaked in.

Kimbo was their mascot. He'd been run over by a car and his back legs looked like twigs, but he'd survived and Buba and Mimi believed he was their establishment's guardian angel. He liked to wander among the tables and rub himself against the legs of visitors.

Suddenly, the man twitched as if struck by an electric shock, and before Buba knew what was happening, Kimbo gave out a piercing yelp. Only now did she hear the gunshot and saw that the man was holding a pistol and shaking all over. Kimbo lay on the cement floor kicking his legs, and a pool of blood formed under his head. The man sat back, put the gun on the table and drained his whisky. Mimi threw herself towards the dog. With her black, permed curls and powdered face, she looked like a character from some silly soap opera.

The man took a wad of German marks from the front pocket of his camouflage jacket, pulled a few from underneath the elastic band, put them on the table and looked into Buba's eyes.

'No,' Buba whispered, 'no.'

She looked at his heavy hand pressing down on the banknotes, his broken fingernails, and she looked at the dying Kimbo. The man opened his mouth to say something, then gave up. He picked up the gun again and pulled Buba by the elbow. She gripped the edge of the table. Mimi went quiet on the floor.

Two more gunshots rang out in the bar. Mimi's curls enveloped Kimbo, and Buba's blond head fell on the table.

The man went behind the bar, poured himself another glass and walked heavily back to his table. His glass was just an inch away from Buba's twitching lips.

'I'm coming, Mummy,' he mumbled in a hoarse voice that cut into the roar of passing lorries. 'But I don't even have a present for you. Could have brought you a cartridge shell. Ha ha ha ha. A hundred shells for flowerpots. A garden full of shells.'

A chill had come over the bar, and the traffic along the motorway had quietened down. The man stroked Buba's prickly head, then went over to Mimi and kneeled down and stroked her blood-caked black curls. He pulled the dog's ear by way of farewell, tied the laces of his heavy boots, then got up, ruffled his hair and without looking back he left 'Las Vegas'.

The Longest Dance

ON SUNDAY EVENING, PEPA WAS JUST OUT OF THE SHOWER and going to bed with a novel called *Blondes Don't Cry*, when the doorbell rang. She checked that her hair was dry and went to open the door in her t-shirt and undies. As she crossed the hall-way, her long naked thighs were like fish gliding at the bottom of the big murky mirror.

It was Yassen.

'I told you not to call me any more,' Pepa said.

Yassen was unshaven and had the look of someone who slept at the railway station. He looked down at the doormat and didn't say anything. Then he took out a half-empty water bottle from his jacket.

'I brought you a present,' he said without lifting his head.

'I can see,' Pepa said.

With his free hand he tried to lean on the door frame and failed. Pepa realised he was drunk.

'Come in,' she said.

He placed the bottle on the table and sat in his favourite caved-in armchair. Yassen seemed to relax and sober up a bit. He brought out cigarettes and matches from his pockets and ceremoniously lit up.

Pepa brought two glasses, poured some vodka into them, sat opposite him on the couch and took a sip. Yassen drained his glass at once and poured himself some more. Now he looked better. He was sitting there looking at her and smoking.

Pepa had another drink.

'Look,' she said. 'Finish your drink and leave, please.'

Yassen drained his vodka as if it were water and smiled. His bad teeth made him look as if he had a wreath of thorns in his mouth.

'Fine. But I have a request. For a dance. One last dance.'

Pepa noticed that it was nearly midnight. She put on a Deep Purple cassette and pressed the play button.

'OK,' she said. 'But promise that you won't call me any more.'

'I won't,' Yassen said.

She got up, went to him, waited for him to rise and put her hands on his shoulders.

On Monday morning, Pepa was late for work at the hairdresser's salon. She couldn't remember when Yassen had left.

She was working like an automaton and just waiting for it to be five o'clock so she could go home and sleep. When she turned around to look at the wall clock, she saw Yassen standing in the doorway. He was washed and dressed up like the conductor of a symphony orchestra. He wore an expensive black suit, a perfect fit, and his tie glittered on his snow-white shirt like a bed of crocus flowers. Avoiding her eyes, he sat in the chair.

'I want you to shave me,' he said. 'My hands shake and I'll cut myself if I do it.'

'We don't have shaving equipment any more. If you like, I can just tidy your beard with the electric clipper.'

'No, I want you to shave me. I have an important invitation tonight. I have to be impeccable.'

'Well, I can't help you.'

'I knew you'd try to wriggle out of it. So I brought everything you need.'

Yassen reached inside his jacket pocket and took out an old-fashioned foldable Solingen razor with an ebony handle and a bronze-stubbed brush. Plus a tube of 'Karo' shaving cream, a popular brand.

'I think that's all we need. I hope you haven't turned off the hot water yet.'

'I haven't,' Pepa said.

She picked up a clean sheet from the cupboard and wrapped it around his neck, then placed a clean towel over it, bent his face to the sink and wetted it with warm water, squeezed out the shaving brush and started soaping him up. Then she sterilised the razor with some alcohol and started scraping the foam from his face.

'You're not going to call me any more, are you?' she said when she'd shaved half of his face. He looked at her in the mirror with a serious expression on his clownish half-white, half-blue face and nodded.

In five minutes, Pepa was done. She tilted his head to the sink again to wash off the smooth cheeks, dried him with the towel and went over to the other work station to pick up some cologne.

When she came back, it took her a while to work out what that huge red thing was, spreading down the sheet. Then the eyes in the mirror became murky and violet. They looked at her from some ecstatic, foggy, disappearing galaxy of love.

Then the head fell back and the blood spurted out.

The Little Rubbish Collector

ONE DAY, AVOIDING EACH OTHER'S EYES, GERRY AND HER mother went out into the street and started lifting the lids of rubbish bins. They had tied two big cardboard boxes to the sides of the wheelchair. Gerry rummaged in the bins, and her mother browsed through the loot and decreed in her screeching voice what was to be taken. People really did throw away the most incredible things, and Gerry had fun with it. In just a week she had acquired a doll and a teddy bear. The doll was shorn like a soldier, and the teddy bear had no eyes, but Gerry was delighted because she had never had proper toys.

Soon enough they stopped caring about what people thought of them. Meanwhile, they'd found an iron and a hoover which Uncle Gosho repaired, after which they sold them quite profitably to some Albanians on the black market. For the first time in ages, a smile came over Mum's face, and Gerry used the opportunity to show off the dress she'd nicked from a washing line. It had ribbon-thin straps and was zipped at the front, and although it had a few cigarette burns, Gerry loved it.

Her mother looked at her for a long time, then lit a cigarette with trembling fingers, inhaled deeply and started crying. It didn't last, though. She suddenly started laughing, wiped her eyes with Varban's big hanky with the American flag and asked Gerry for a glass of cognac. When she'd drunk it, she pulled Gerry to her and they talked for a long time about life and how, God willing, they might get wealthy one day, and then Mum would send Gerry to school again and later, she might even become a fashion model – why not? She was pretty and long-legged, just like a model. And who knows, perhaps Dad would call from America and invite them over.

'And then you'll buy me a big fur coat, won't you,' her mother said. 'I've always wanted a real fur coat. Varban promised me one, but you know, I wasn't lucky there.'

The next day, Gerry put on the same dress and her mother didn't comment, she just told her to hurry up with the paper and the cardboard because Gregor from the recycled paper depot wasn't going to wait for ever.

Gerry was scared of Gregor. He always left her mother in her wheelchair out in the courtyard, and ordered Gerry to come up to the wagon to sign off the invoice logs. Inside the wagon it was dark and smelled of dog. While Gerry stared at the log, Gregor would stand right next to her and start breathing hard, like a blocked sink.

Now he weighed up the paper quickly and ordered Gerry to come up the iron ladder. His eyes were constantly on her. When the door slammed behind them, Gregor grabbed her with his massive hands and shoved his raspy face into her neck.

Gerry froze. She knew she shouldn't piss him off because Mum said that all their income depended on him. She stood there for a while and put up with it, while pressing her legs tightly together. Then she had the presence of mind to tell Gregor that she'd come back tomorrow, but without her mother. He let her go, his eyes still on her. His mouth was shiny like a frying pan. Feeling all slimy, Gerry jumped down and quickly started pushing the wheelchair.

In the afternoon, she took her mother to see Penka the seamstress. The two women liked to chat over a glass of cognac. Gerry promised to come and pick her up in the evening, as usual. Then she ran out.

This was her favourite time of the day. She walked down the boulevards and looked in the shop windows. She imagined herself in this dress or that, and she saw herself as a fashion model. Then everyone would crawl at her feet.

Suddenly, as if by accident, she found herself at the foreigner's shop. The foreigner was sitting in a chair outside, but when he saw her, he politely invited her in. He was old, like Uncle Gosho, but he had a nice moustache and smelled good. He brought out a box of Turkish delight and opened it. He looked at Gerry as she crammed in one piece of Turkish delight after another. He smiled and nodded his head like a big, friendly horse. Then he asked in his broken Bulgarian whether she'd like him to give her some new clothes. Gerry didn't know what to say, although she really wanted the new clothes, and the foreigner understood her because next thing, he turned the key in the lock and took her to the back of the shop. He left her to rummage in a big pile of clothes, and when she finally chose a denim tunic with silver buttons he simply reached out and pulled down the zip of her dress. Gerry stood still because she was afraid he might change his mind about the expensive gift. He removed her dress, then brought a bottle of perfume and sprayed her all over. The perfume was so overpowering she felt dizzy. Then he slowly undressed himself, all the while looking into her eyes. His chest was strong and well defined and covered in a carpet of curly white hairs. When he leaned over her, Gerry went quiet because his moustache tickled her. The foreigner slowly laid her down on the couch.

Later, she got up and went inside the cupboard-sized toilet to wash herself. She quickly put on the denim tunic. Then she realised that she couldn't explain it to her mother, so she asked the foreigner for money instead. The money came in a big wad and seemed like a fortune. She counted it after she'd left the shop, and started running. It was more money than she and her mother could make from collecting rubbish in half a year.

The next day, during their rubbish rounds, Gerry found a shoe box wrapped in brown paper. Money, lots of money tumbled out of the box and into her mother's lap. Gerry was happy to see her mother jumping up and down with joy in her wheelchair. She convinced her to go home straight away. She poured her two glasses of cognac, after which her mother fell asleep. Gerry quickly washed with cold water and ran off to the foreigner's shop again. There was only one thing on her mind: the pile of money, and how it would grow bigger and bigger, and her mother would have a fur coat. Gerry would go back to school and after she graduated, she'd become a fashion model. Because Mum said that she was pretty and long-legged like a model.

Then finally, the two of them would be able to catch the plane and go to that country whose flag is colourful like a hanky. And as Gerry walks down the catwalk, casting glamorous glances this way and that, and her mother, clad in a fur coat, claps from the first row – just then, from some corner of the hall, manically pushing his way through the crowd with his elbows, comes Daddy.

March

ON SUNDAYS, IF THE WEATHER IS NICE, WE LET SOME OF
the lesser loonies out for a walk.

They do endless rounds in the small park of the hospital,
shake the branches of the trees, sit on the benches and smoke.

At six o'clock everyone has to be back upstairs.

During the seven-thirty medication rounds, the evening
nurse discovered that Milen was missing from the men's ward,
and Olya from the women's.

Milen was a young soldier who'd been with us for six months,
and the outlook wasn't good. At the beginning, he was pretty
bad. He'd stand to attention whenever someone walked by, or
start shooting indiscriminately with his imaginary machine gun
while making excellent imitation machine-gun sounds with his
mouth. Then he got better – the medication was having an effect

– and Milen became more or less like everybody else here. His vacant eyes and shuffling gait were a sign of his defeat.

Things were a bit different with Olya. We had to watch her. She was forever trying to lure the male orderlies into the bathroom, then she'd shed her clothes in no time and start making lewd movements with her body. Sometimes we had to tie her down.

We called the police at once. They were used to us, but promised to send out a patrol car anyway. Our patients often wandered beyond the hospital grounds. Usually, the police found them around the National Palace of Culture or down in the subway, or by the water fountains outside the nightclub.

Around nine o'clock, the patrol called the head doctor to say they'd found them. They brought them in – both still wearing their green hospital gowns, smiling radiantly. Olya had plaited her hair into small braids, and Milen was wearing his thick army belt. The policeman told us how he'd found them outside some big black shop window, holding hands and periodically walking away from it, then marching back towards it, and as soon as they reached the window, they'd simultaneously start writing something on it with their fingers.

'What were you doing there?' the head doctor asked them.

Olya looked down shyly, but Milen didn't blink.

'We got married,' he said. 'And this young general was our best man.'

Olya giggled.

The policeman carefully and stiffly removed Milen's hand from his shoulder.

'Goodbye,' he said. 'Let's hope we won't see each other again tonight.'

Around eleven, the two wards went quiet. Only the fags of the dedicated smokers flickered in the bathroom. I brought out the bucket and the rag, unlocked the door leading to the hallway where the busts of distinguished psychiatrists stood between the male and the female wards, and called Milen.

'You won't get away with it,' I yelled at him. 'Finish your fag and start cleaning. I want the corridor to shine. Not a dry spot on the mosaic.'

The night-shift doctor came out of the male ward at this point, crossed the hallway past Milen, who stood to attention, and went up the stairs to his office. A second after his door slammed, the female door was opened and the orderly Auntie Velichka appeared. Behind her was Olya's beautiful face.

'I want everything to shine!' Auntie Velichka screeched angrily, without even looking at us. 'There's dust on the radiators. There's dust on the window sills. You're not going anywhere until you're finished.'

After that, Auntie Velichka and I went back inside our wards. Through the half-open door, I saw Milen drop the bucket, grab Olya's hand and they rushed down the stairs. There was a huge lecture auditorium downstairs for the medical students.

It was March. Thousands of stars must have flickered through the cathedral-like windows of the auditorium. I saw the stars too, one floor up, through the kitchen window. The phone rang.

'Is that the in-laws?' said Auntie Velichka on the line. 'We mustn't forget to wake up the newly-weds tomorrow morning.'

'Well, if we forget, the students will do it for us,' I smiled and put the phone down. I propped my head up on the table, and once again I thought about Olya and Milen, how handsome they were. I thought about her plaited hair and his smart leather belt.

Yes, it was March, and outside in the hospital garden I could hear the drawn-out wailing of cats.

The Slaughter of the Rooster

THE OLD GEOGRAPHY TEACHER PETER PRESOLSKI WAS SIT-
ting in a chair in the kitchen and looking out of the window. It
was a lovely winter's day. The light made bright squares on the
floorboards and the teacher had to squint.

The old geography teacher retired two months ago. In the
morning, when the postwoman brought the paper, he greedily
pulled it out of her hands, leaned on the stove and read it from
cover to cover, but even after that it was only ten o'clock. Now
Presolski was waiting for lunchtime, so he could feed the hens.
This was his only chore during the day – to feed the six hens and
the crested rooster. His eyes wandered idly over the kitchen
walls. His old habits were hanging there like broken cobwebs.
His unpolished shoes were by the door. His unironed trousers
were on the chest of drawers. His cheeks were covered with silver

bristles. But the biggest calamity was his geography teacher's memory. His memory usefully produced the names of faraway countries, mountains, rivers and seas, the fruits of thirty years of teaching. Now, these names catapulted him to different far-flung corners of the globe. The terrifying speed of his travels made him see long flashes of light. His lips moved to these names which he'd uttered thousands of times in the classroom. It was like a daily prayer: Niagara Falls and the Nile, the Gobi desert and the Dead Sea, the Mariana Plate and Tierra del Fuego, the Strait of Magellan and Kilimanjaro, Texas and Ontario Lake, Labrador and the Gulf stream, Norway the homeland of Christmas trees, and Kamchatka, the Bering Strait and the Sahara. There were lots more beautiful exotic names like that, and they all flickered in Peter Presolski's memory like diamonds which he no longer had the right to touch.

For thirty years, the geography teacher had travelled to the nearby town where he taught his subject at a high school, and now the midday winter sun coming through the window and shining straight in his eyes somehow felt like a blasphemy.

It was lunchtime at last. Peter Presolski got up, pulled the pot of boiling water away from the element, poured the water into a bucket for the hens' feed and went off with the bucket down the cinder-covered path. The hens saw him from afar and perched on the metal netting of the coop. The rooster stood behind them, keeping a curved eye on the bucket. The teacher

poured the feed into a severed tyre and stepped aside. The rooster kept his cool a few more seconds, then he gave in and rushed
to the tyre and started gulping down the hot bran.

Soon, the tyre was squeaky clean. The hens left their feast one
by one, and started grooming themselves lethargically in the sun.
The rooster pulled away too. He cast an eye on his brood, chose
a hen which that day looked particularly attractive to him, cir-
cled her while his wing scratched the dirt, then he pecked her
quickly on the head and jumped on top of her. It was over in a
few seconds. Then the proud rooster jumped to the ground
heavily, and while the hen was shaking her wings, he did a little
circle before her, his wing dragging on the dirt gallantly, then he
crouched, stretched his tough neck and crowed sonorously. At
once, other roosters took up, and soon the whole village rang
with cocks' crows. But you could tell that nothing out of the
ordinary was happening from the way that the hens indiffer-
ently dug the earth. Indeed, soon enough the hoarse voices
burned out and a deadly quiet fell over the winter afternoon.

The teacher felt that he was on the brink of a major rev-
elation, that any minute now he would make an important
discovery. He stood waiting like this and looking at the muddy
mess around him, the brick chicken coop, the fairy-tale blue sky,
the chimney smoke coming out of the houses like prayer… But
then the moment was over and the retired teacher turned back
and walked to the house with the empty bucket.

In the evening, when the retired geography teacher's wife came back from work, she saw a tin basin by the doorstep, and inside it was the naked, plucked body of the rooster. The teacher was sitting on a stump by the basin, looking straight ahead. His wife tried to make him talk, but he wouldn't say anything, and when he finally tried to speak, only a desperate gurgle came out of his throat.

The Girl of My Dreams

A SINGLE RED WINDOW IS LIT UP AT NIGHT IN THE HOUSE opposite. Most evenings, come midnight, a taxi pulls up at its gates. A woman steps out of the taxi, enters the heavy double gates and disappears into the courtyard.

I don't know when she leaves because I usually nod off at dawn, exhausted from waiting. I wake up around lunchtime. Now the red window is dark, the double gates are locked with a chain and behind the wire fence, two enormous pure-bred German Shepherds are running about.

They built the three-storey house in a single summer. It stands at the end of a long, narrow yard fenced off by a two-metre high wire fence. Although the house is complete, it is obvious that only one room is inhabited – the red-lit room on the second floor.

During the day, there is no sign of life around the house. The dogs greet passers-by with rabid barking. They must tie them up at night, and unlock the door. I can tell from the way the woman arriving in the taxi opens the door freely, and walks up the tiled pathway to the house.

Sometimes I wonder if these women ever leave the house. Perhaps something happens to them, and the new ones that arrive don't know what's in store for them. At one or two in the morning, one thinks sinister thoughts.

To be fair to me, the house does look sinister with its locked-up, barbed-wire courtyard, the raving dogs behind the fence and the two powerful searchlights that hit the tiled pathway at night.

And there's the taxi again. I hear the engine, and I hear some voices, male and female, then the uneven click of high heels on the cement tiles.

Tonight I've decided not to fall asleep and to find out at any cost what goes on there. I drink coffee non-stop, rub my eyes and keep them on the house. I live across the street and have a clear view of everything.

As usual, I wake up at around eleven the next day, puffy-faced and dazed with sleep because I've spent the entire night in the armchair by the window. I make myself a few strong coffees, smoke five cigarettes and I'm feeling better. I take another look at the house. The red window has gone dark, the double gate is chained up and the dogs are untied.

At midnight, my doorbell rings. I go downstairs. A young woman is standing in the doorway. She's gorgeous, with a big, brightly painted mouth, artificial eyelashes that flutter like nocturnal butterfly wings and her head is shorn and bleached downy-gold. She wears violet eye make-up, and artificial freckles sparkle on her cheeks. Beneath her overcoat, I glimpse a tight silvery bodysuit and black fishnet stockings held up with suspenders, revealing a few inches of smooth, naked thigh.

So that's who you are, I think to myself, and step aside to let her in. Her heels tap on the floor tiles and then up the stairs. I follow behind like a sleepwalker. She wastes no time in the bedroom. She casts off the overcoat, puts one leg up on the bedside table and rolls down the black cobweb of stocking, then drops it on the floor and does the same with the other one. Then she slips out of the bodysuit like a snake shedding a skin and stands before me buck naked. Her skin is the colour of peaches.

I'm shaking all over, incredulous that the girl of my dreams is so close. Fortunately, she takes things in hand and comes over to me, stands on tiptoe and embraces me. She undoes my belt buckle and soon, I'm naked too. My peachy guest takes me by the hand and pushes me down on the bed and whispers to me to be quiet. She kisses me on the mouth, then her lips travel downwards. Seconds before the roof falls in, she meets my eyes, lifts herself up, opens her beautiful legs and takes me in.

Her body starts to move up and down, her collarbones shine

119

with moisture like marble, her eyes are open and follow me unblinkingly. She tenses up and her irises dilate, and then the ceiling falls over me, soft and warm like ashes.

Moments later, she dresses silently and leaves. I don't see her off because I'm too sleepy. When I get up the following day at midday, I drink coffee and smoke for ages. I don't even feel like looking outside. The secret is out in the open. But I'm not complaining. A woman like that can come to you only in your dreams.

Finally, I glance at the house opposite out of habit.

The wire fence has been pulled down and the dogs are running freely in the street. Just before I look away, I catch sight of someone at the red window, someone who's observing me.

In the evening, I get ready. I shower, comb my hair, put on my favourite clothes – the velvet jacket, the grey polo-neck, the pressed trousers – and burning with impatience, I sit down to wait. The dogs are nowhere to be seen. It's high time for another visit. But midnight comes and there is no visitor. Around two, tired of waiting, I clean out the ashtray and go to bed.

In the morning, I rush to the window. Down in the street there are whirlwinds of dust. In a moment, the two dogs come charging along with crazed howls. When a taxi pulls up, I rush down the stairs like a madman. She's chosen a strange time to visit, true, but it doesn't matter any more – what matters is that I'll see her again now. I fling the door open before the bell rings.

A taxi driver stands in the doorway. It's only now I realise that it's not morning at all. It's the dead of night, and what confused me was the bright light of the searchlights pointed straight at my house. The air is so heated from the light of the projectors that I begin to sweat.

'Will you please settle your bill?' the taxi driver says. 'Here it is.' And he hands me a piece of paper with a six-figure amount on it.

On each side of him the dogs are breathing heavily, their tongues hanging out.

They come up to his waist. Their eyes are on me.

Brother of Mine

ONE DAY, A BIG FISH CAME INTO THE BOXERS' GYM, FLANKED
by two bodyguards. His face was smooth like a baby's, and his
eyes were sad like those of a tinned sardine, but the gym bosses
and trainers snapped to attention and the sweat poured down
their necks. George Peshev heard the big fish quietly say his
name, and then he heard the trainers heap praises on him,
George. Then Mr Big Fish called him over, squeezed his hand
and gave him a big wad of banknotes held together by an elastic
band. When Big Fish was gone, George understood that he had
to use this money to deck himself out in the kind of clothes that
would make people think he was a junior lecturer at university.

And so began George Peshev's career with Big Fish. Every
morning, they sent him to a private shooting gallery to train,
and in the end he was so good he could put out a candle from

sixty paces with a single shot. At that point, they shoved a gun under his arm, another in his belt and he went on the payroll of the Big Fish.

His boss's job consisted of driving around in his Mercedes and stopping off at certain places to chat to certain people. From about lunchtime, he started to drink, and if he overdid it, it was George's job to pick up the remains of his personality. On Saturday, George had a day off. That's when he usually went to see his brother Ivailo. They'd go out on the balcony, sit on stools, drink beer, and his brother would bring him up to date with the affairs of the world. His brother had always been the brains of the family. Since he was a high-school student he'd been interested in computers, and now he had his own successful software business.

Then one Saturday, the boss sent him off on a job in the countryside with Rocky and the Monkey. They arrived in a small provincial town around midday, and parked the Mercedes outside the nightclub in the main square. The establishment was closed. The three of them went in through the staff entrance, and found the owner in the process of making tiny braids in the hair of a blonde babe. Rocky and the Monkey locked the babe in the toilet and stuffed her mouth with toilet paper. Then they tied the man to a chair. Then they boiled a whole litre of coffee and started pouring it directly into his mouth through a funnel. The man screamed, and as soon as they untied him, he signed the paperwork that the Monkey had thoughtfully brought along. Four hours later, they were back in Sofia. The Monkey handed the boss a little leather case stuffed with money. The boss praised George, patted his neck with a hand soft as a drowned cat and told him to go and rest.

George's brother was down in the dumps that Saturday. After the third beer, Ivailo loosened up and told his brother that he was having trouble with some guys. George insisted that if he kept having trouble with those guys, he must call him. He looked at his brother's bespectacled face and the muscles of his shoulders twitched.

The following week, George went around the country with Rocky and the Monkey. It was the same story every time and all went well. By the end of the week, it was practically raining little leather cases. There was only one stubborn case where Rocky and the Monkey had to resort to their pump-action shotguns. In another case, when they tied up the men, they were so caught up they forgot all about the coffee and went straight to plan B – breaking fingers. The men signed the paperwork at once. True, the signatures came out a bit crooked, but who cares.

The boss welcomed them back with a big smile, took the money and gave George a Sofia address. He instructed him to act as usual, and added that this was going to be his christening. Rocky and the Monkey sat on each side of the boss and played with the matchsticks in their mouths.

It was a business address. George went in, and there stood his brother. Ivailo was glad to see him, made him some tea and added that things were all right for the time being and that nobody had called for him. George shuffled about the office, looked at the computers and left without finishing his tea. He drove like a maniac. He went to his boss and explained that there had been a mistake. The address was Ivailo's office, and Ivailo was his brother.

The boss took a sip from his drink and scratched his ear. Rocky and the Monkey got up, spat out the matchsticks and unbuttoned their jackets. The boss looked at George for a while with a puzzled expression, then he became so sad you'd think he'd just seen his own obituary. There are no brothers and sisters in this job, he said. An order was an order. Now will George be a good boy, and go back and finish his job.

The boxer's right-hand blow caught him right before the full stop of his sentence. The boss fell into an enormous pot plant and started writhing like a worm at the end of a hook. Rocky and the Monkey fired at once. George felt no pain and saw no blood.

At his funeral, there were at least thirty black limousines. Rocky and the Monkey carried his coffin, helped by two other gorillas with stubbly, funereal faces. The boss wore dark glasses and sat inside the car throughout. When it was over, he called for the brother of the deceased and handed him a fat wad of banknotes held by an elastic band. He said he deeply mourned Georgie Peshev. He'd never have such an excellent employee again. He also said that if he, Ivailo, or anyone else in his family ever ran into trouble, they could always count on him. There was no such thing as impossible for him, the boss concluded, and sorrowfully patted George's brother on the cheek.

Saint Ana

THEY BROUGHT THE FIVE BOYS AT SEVEN IN THE MORNING.
Auntie Ani and I hadn't yet finished our coffee. The two orderlies slapped them down on the stone tables one by one, then
leaned on the wall to catch their breath.

'Rocky and his people,' the tall, browless orderly said. 'They
were keeping girls in the Hotel Victoria. The whole eleventh
floor was theirs. Not any more. Poor girls, though. New masters
are always worse.'

'Apparently it was a hell of a mess,' said the short one.

Then they folded up their stretcher and padded noiselessly
up the stairs.

The Kalashnikov bullets had turned the boys into foam
rubber. The shooter or shooters had clearly had a rucksack full
of bullets, and plenty of time to reload. The four boys in jackets

were shorn, and the one in a suit had shoulder-length blond hair. One of them was wearing a watch that had been ground to a pulp by the bullets – perhaps he'd tried to hide behind it. Another one had worn a belt whose buckle had come out through his back. The blond one had a big ear-to-ear bullet smile embroidered on his face.

Auntie Ani poured some medicinal alcohol into a tin jug and made me drink it, then threw some gloves at me. We worked silently for about three hours. At the end, she unwound the big, python-like hose, stuck one end onto the sink tap and washed everything clean with the thunderous water jet – the naked boys, the tables, the floor. Then she wiped her hands and went to make a phone call. Five minutes later, we heard a knock. She opened the morgue door, heavy as a submarine lid, took five identical packages and closed the door again. In each package there was a black suit, a white shirt, socks and a pair of new shoes, size forty-five.

We worked for two more hours. When Auntie Ani finished, the boys looked like high-school graduates who were sound asleep after the night of the ball. Her talent for turning corpses into beautiful dead people knew no bounds. The only thing was, the shoes were a tad big for the blond one. I was beginning to shiver. I went over to the sink and vomited. Then I washed my hands and face, and, holding up my left eyelid with two fingers, so it wouldn't twitch, I looked at Auntie Ani. She looked back at me. The smiley one seemed to move on his table. Auntie Ani went behind the curtain and came back with a small icon, five candles and a pair of scissors. She hung the icon on a nail, lit the candles, dripped some wax and stuck them to the cement floor and stood there for a while, whispering something to herself. Then she spat on her fingers and put the candles out, put the little icon away and cut off a lock of the blond boy's hair. She took everything away, and when she came out, she said: 'Now let's go for a fag.'

We went out into the corridor, sat by the small table and lit up. While we smoked, the two orderlies slid down the stairs like ghosts. The browless one carried the canvas stretcher over one shoulder. When the last boy had gone up the worn amber-coloured stairs on the stretcher, the chair underneath Auntie Ani squeaked.

'Why did you cut off a lock of his hair?' I asked.

'To give to his mother,' she said, all matter-of-fact, then suddenly her face shrivelled up and darkened like burning paper, and her massive shoulders began to shake uncontrollably.

The Pawn Shop

THE LITTLE DOORBELL TINKLED AND KALIN BANDEROV raised his eyes from the crossword he'd been wrestling with all morning – it was big, like the map of the former Soviet Union. The visitor was an old woman, transparent like a cobweb and so skinny she was practically buckling under the weight of her big wooden coat buttons. Kalin Banderov took her measure with one look and could barely hide his annoyance. He saw the likes of her in spades these days. With desperate determination, from the unfathomable folds of time, these poor people managed to produce objects that had no value whatsoever except to them, for sentimental reasons – hair clips, thimbles, purses, little doilies with kissing pigeons, inkwells, cigarette-holders, duck feathers, tin bracelets, imitation gold – and tried to pawn them or even sell them outright. Kalin Banderov would lose his nerve and scream at them. These wretches couldn't understand that the decades of sentiment with which they'd invested their possessions were not worth a single penny.

The old woman shuffled timidly towards the antique walnut desk where Kalin Banderov sat. As she shuffled, she tried to apologise for the inconvenience.

'This is a pawn shop, isn't it?' she asked, and stood at the far end of the vast desk. She was so small she looked like a porcelain statuette placed on top of the table, murky and cracked with age.

'Yes, madam.'

'I'm sorry, I didn't hear you.'

'I said, yes, this is a pawn shop!'

'And what items do you accept here?'

'All sorts, madam.'

'Do you accept old items, by any chance?'

'It depends, madam. It's best if I see what you have in mind.'

'What sums do you offer, if you don't mind me asking?'

Kalin Banderov was tempted just to throw her out there and then, but decided to play at being polite a bit longer.

'If your item is new or in spotless condition, madam, we agree on a sum which reflects its real price, and then I'd give you – but again, I repeat that it would depend on the condition of the item – I'd give you between ten and fifty per cent of that sum. The time limit for covering that loan is thirty days, plus a free three-day period. If you come within that time limit, but you can't buy the item off, you will have the opportunity to extend your loan by another month, in return for another small sum, of course. And if you still can't buy it off, it becomes the property of the shop. We have sample contracts where these conditions are laid out. The contract is signed by each party.'

The old woman listened carefully and in the dark, violet pits of her sockets, her eyes flickered or perhaps watered, like two tiny mirrors.

'I have something here,' she said.

Kalin Banderov felt the muscles of his legs flex, as if he were about to pounce. The heavy gold chain on his right wrist lay flat on the polished surface of the desk like an anaconda. The likelihood of this old woman coming up with something truly valuable was one in a thousand, but the hunter's instinct still made his nostrils twitch.

The old woman reached inside the threadbare pocket of her coat and extracted something wrapped in lots of newspaper. Slowly, with shaking hands, she unwrapped it. She took in a sharp breath, and placed down on the desk an indescribably gorgeous gold Omega watch.

Kalin Banderov knew a thing or two about valuables. He bought them off immediately, even if the owners didn't suspect their true value, and through his own well-developed channels he sold them on the black market in the West, where their value went up tenfold.

'This watch belonged to my husband,' the old woman said melodiously, as if she'd told this story so many times, it had turned into a song. 'He had it from his father. On the inside of the cap there is an inscription, you can see it. My late husband, may he rest in peace, was a doctor. He had a taste for beautiful things. You should have seen how dignified he looked when he carried this watch in his pocket. When he wanted to know the time, he would get up – he never did it sitting – and he'd click the lid open and look at it with delight, for at least one minute. I always felt that when he looked at this watch adoringly, the whole world adored him in turn.'

While he listened to the old woman distractedly, Kalin Banderov caressed the precious watch in his hands and was already making mental calculations in dollars. He clicked the little lid and it bounced up elegantly. On the inside, there was a laconic inscription. Kalin Banderov read it once, then another time and another.

'To my son Kalin Banderov – with hope and faith.' He didn't get this at all. When he raised his eyes, the old woman wasn't there. The strange thing is, the bell hadn't even tinkled.

A Day in the Life of Emma

GRANDPA BEGGAR SAT ON THE STEPS OF THE CHURCH AND started arranging his worldly goods around him: the crutches, the plastic water bottle, the piece of polystyrene, the money tin which he carefully placed on top of the polystyrene as if on a pedestal. He was all set now. His face was the colour of an old horse saddle, and his beard was silver.

This was exactly how a beggar should look, in Emma's view. Every morning, he performed this ritual with fresh inspiration and remarkable thoroughness.

'God bless you,' he said hoarsely to the first passer-by who dropped a coin in the tin. The coin rang so loudly it echoed around the entire square. Emma squeezed her eyes from sheer joy.

They were ready to begin the day.

By ten o'clock, the autumn sun had warmed them up a bit. The first tourists appeared. Emma adjusted the straps of her heavy accordion on her shoulders and began to play. She knew only two tunes because she was only eleven, but the people passing through constantly changed, so they didn't know that.

At eleven o'clock, Emma took off the straps of the accordion, collected the money from the old bowler hat in front of her, stretched like a cat and looked towards the bench in the little park at the edge of the square, where her father normally sat. Yet again, he wasn't there. Emma felt like crying.

In the morning, he'd combed a path into her hair, plaited it and helped her carry the heavy accordion from the wagon where they lived to the church steps, and when she had taken her place, he'd crouched before her and broken down. She'd looked at his murky, bloodshot eyes, his bristly stubble, his ragged shirt collar, his coat shiny with filth and had kept nodding.

Finally, he sighed and got up, and with a proud walk he went over to his bench. He hadn't lost his proud walk yet. Emma took secret pleasure from her father's proud walk. This here was her father, no less.

Then Grandpa Beggar turned up, and she concentrated on him.

Around lunchtime, a flock of Japanese tourists flooded the square. They looked like exotic birds with their strange twittering and colourful clothes. They recorded everything with their camcorders – the park, the square, the church – dropped some banknotes in her hat and in the beggar's tin, while Emma desperately wanted to take a peek in one of the video-cameras. She wanted it so badly that she had to kill it at once and quickly play the tunes, first one, then the other.

At two o'clock the paedophile arrived. Actually, Emma didn't know that's what he was, but she did know that she really, really wanted this man to turn suddenly into a puddle. The paedophile stroked her cheek, then slid his index finger down her thin neck, then down her spine, crushed her ear lobe for a while and tried to talk to her, but Emma just gritted her teeth and played like crazy, first one tune, then the other.

Finally, the paedophile came to with a start, as if struck by an electric shock, looked around, wiped the beads of sweat over his lip, dropped a sweet in her hat and walked away in his funny, giraffe-like walk. Emma waited for him to disappear, put the accordion down on the steps, grabbed the sweet and crunched it at once.

At five, Grandpa Beggar collected his worldly goods once again, then dragged himself on his arse towards her, took out a banknote, smoothed it out and placed it in Emma's hat, then gave her a little bow and dragged himself back to his place where he hoisted himself up on his crutches and went clattering, tap-tap, across the square.

At six, her father finally turned up. He wasn't lurching about, but she knew it from the colour of his face. It was blue, and his eyes were made of glass. He picked up the hat, shook the money out of it and put it in his coat pocket, slung the accordion over his shoulder and pulled her hand. Emma knew that now was not the time to object to anything, and she ran after him.

In twenty minutes they reached Chavdar Bridge, passed underneath it, crossed three railway lines without checking for oncoming trains, and her father kept pulling at her hand and Emma kept running faster and tripping over, until they reached their wagon and her father flung the accordion into the echoing cave. You mustn't do it like that, Emma wanted to say, it will break and then what are we going to do when it breaks, but she didn't say anything, and then her father grabbed her and shoved her inside the wagon too, and climbed up himself.

In the night, Emma dreamed her usual dream: the train drives over her father's body and cuts it in two, but he's OK from the waist up and he just finds himself a couple of excellent shiny crutches and sits in the place of Grandpa Beggar on the steps, and in the evening, before they go home, he crawls up to her, tap-tap, tap-tap, and puts a sweet inside her hat. Not just any sweet though – the biggest sweet in the world.

Big as a church.

Orlando

'YOUNG WOMAN,' THE OLD TRAMP SAID, 'STOP BEING A PAIN.'

The monkey squatted next to him on the ground. She was tied to his wrist with a thick chain. Her beautiful gold-specked eyes watched the approaching boy anxiously.

'Want another beer?' The girl stood next to his chair with two big plastic mugs of draft. She wore skinny black jeans and chunky trainers. The old man nodded with dignity. 'What's the monkey's name?' asked the other girl. She was sitting next to him on the pavement. She had long bare legs and a big painted red mouth.

'Christina,' said the old man.

The monkey heard its name and pulled at the chain.

'Young woman,' the tramp told her off.

'Does Christina drink beer?' the red-mouthed girl wanted to know.

'From time to time,' the old man smiled.

The boy took an empty plastic coffee cup and poured some beer into it. The monkey took it carefully with dainty black fingers and delicately took a sip. The girl and the boy screamed with delight.

'Cheers, Christina,' said the old man.

In his ripped old silver alpaca jacket, he looked like a luckless Martian whose spaceship would never leave Earth again.

Dusk was falling. People started to leave the market. The sellers were packing up their stalls and moving stuff back to their car boots. Down the market's main street came the madwoman, lighting discarded cigarette ends, her eyeballs rolling horribly. She was sobering up again, which meant she was on her way to her regular watering hole to share a table with some drunk, then repay him in the disused nearby subway.

After the fourth beer, the old man felt a rush of strength again. He hadn't eaten all day, but the beer took the edge off his hunger.

'What's your name?' the boy asked. His eyes were mercury-black and disconcerting. His shaved head was split by a mane of stiff blond hair, like Achilles' helmet.

'Me?' the old man said, and rubbed his bristly cheek. 'To be honest with you, I can't remember. Sure, I had a name once, but if the name doesn't go with the person, it disappears. The person may walk this sinful earth a while longer, but the name is dead.'

'He's taking the piss.' The boy turned to the girl. 'Did you hear that? He's got no name. I don't like the sound of this.'

'Old man,' the boy shouted in his ear. 'Don't take the piss. Tell me your name or I'm gonna lose it.'

'It's the truth, boy,' the man said, and stared down into his empty plastic cup as if staring into a deep well. 'We're all on our way to Orlandovtsi Cemetery, but I'm right at the front, beating the drums. Pam-param, pam-param. That's what you can call me, if you must. Orlando. Call me Orlando.'

'More beer, Orlando?'

'Yes please,' he said with dignity.

The beer made him feel big and strong. It muted his hunger and made him forget for a moment that he had nowhere to sleep and not a coin in his pocket.

Suddenly, Christina bounced up and bit the boy on the sleeve. The old man pulled her chain back, but she went on the attack again.

'What's wrong with you, hussy,' the old man shouted, and slapped her hard on the head. The monkey shrank under his plastic chair and remained there, cowering.

At dawn, he woke up from the freezing cold. He tried to remember where he was, but couldn't. When he tried to get up, something pulled at his neck. He waited a while then tried again, but that thing kept pulling him down. Then, through the terrible, blinding, yellow fog of his mind, it reached him – his neck was tied with a chain. The other end of the chain was wound around the metal leg of a market stall and locked with a padlock.

'Where's Christina?' He suddenly remembered the monkey. He looked around in desperation, as far as the chain allowed him, but there was no monkey.

Somewhere in the city, a church bell tolled.

The old man fell on the black cement and wept. At some point, the madwoman crawled out of the subway, came up to him, looked at him a while, then reached up with her big, sewage-stinking, hoof-like hand and started to wipe his tears away.

'Don't cry,' she said. 'You know, they been tying me up all my life, and look at me, just fine. We're gonna unlock the chain now, then we'll have some nice beers. It's a day for celebration, old man, we're gonna celebrate. See, the bells are tolling for us today.'

Mother

WHENEVER THE TWINS WERE ADMITTED TO OUR WARD, IT was fun time again. And they were frequent guests. We'd discharge them, and two days later – bang, they're standing in the corridor again, their big, dishevelled block heads bent down guiltily as if to say, We can't help it, we're nuts. I greeted them like old acquaintances – I gave them good pyjamas and tried to find them beds by the window. Here, in the psychiatric hospital, we called them Barny and Fred. They were both beasts, but Barny was a bit more controlled, a bit finer. His brother Fred was a natural disaster. When he lost it, only Barny could contain him. Barny would help me strap Fred down to the bed frame, then he stayed for a long time by his side, stroking his brother's moaning head. Gradually Fred would calm down and drift off. True, the cocktail of drugs the nurses dosed him with on such occasions – Chlorazine, Tizersin, Haloperidol – also played a role. If you gave this to a bull he'd die on the spot – but Fred was fine, the animal. The next morning, he'd lodge himself over the bathroom sink and embark on a series of savage ablutions. And at six thirty on the dot, he and Barny would be the first ones to turn up for breakfast in the canteen – well combed, neat and smart like samurai.

Around eleven in the morning, after the doctor's visit, the twins quietened down. As if by command, they jumped into bed, and there they lay noiselessly like sailing boats in a windless spell.

'Those two are masturbating again,' reported the other patients in the room. I would just shrug. We didn't have injections for that sort of thing.

On the ward we had a nurse called Julia, affectionately known as Juleto, little Julia. She'd just come back from a holiday by the seaside and the thin white uniform she wore over her naked body couldn't hide her dazzling chocolate limbs. Every time Juleto walked past the twins, they seized up and their hot bovine eyes went out of focus. I was always teasing her about it, telling her to watch it with those two, and to have an injection of that terrible cocktail on standby in her pocket. She thought I was hilarious.

Then, one lovely Saturday at the end of summer, while most patients were outside in the courtyard and I was somewhere on the upper floors of the hospital, the twins managed to kidnap

Juleto and lock themselves in the bathroom with her. Fortunately, one of the patients had seen this and dashed off to find me. I gathered a solid contingent and we managed to break the bathroom door down and save Juleto within an inch of the worst happening. She never talked about the ordeal of being in there with the two wild centaurs. While we were tying them down, Barny seemed to have an inkling of something resembling guilt. Not Fred the gorilla, though. Even strapped down, Fred continued to twist and moan, and the straps cracked to bursting under the strain of his animal strength. All he knew was that his toy had been taken away. The other nurses were livid, and jammed into the beastly buttocks such elephantine doses of tranquillisers that I thought they really were going to kick the bucket this time. Nothing of the sort. In the morning, they were first in line for breakfast as if nothing had happened.

A little later, though, Fred had an accident in his pants. Barny gently asked me to unlock the bathroom, so he could clean his brother up. Afterwards, I gave Fred a fresh pair of pyjamas, and Barny shyly asked for one too.

'Mum is coming today,' he said. 'It's Sunday. She always comes on Sunday.'

Their mother arrived at two in the afternoon. I briefly told her what had happened. She pulled me aside and started talking in a sing-song voice, as if reciting something she'd said many times.

'I got married young. My husband worked as a prison guard. He was a big, handsome man, like the twins. When I became pregnant, he was a sweetheart, always trying to help and take the load off me. He never talked about his work, but I could see that it really took it out of him. One morning, he came back from night shift, went into the kitchen and just stood there for ages, white as a sheet. His hair was plastered to his forehead with sweat. I got up to make him breakfast. Suddenly, he asked me to pour him a glass of rakia. He drank it, refilled his glass and asked me to leave the kitchen. God, how I wish I hadn't. I'd just shut the door when I heard the gunshot. How I wish I hadn't. He had shot himself in the mouth. I wailed like a wolf for three days. On the third day, I felt the contractions and went into hospital. The same night, I gave birth to the twins.'

The woman went quiet, then asked me to let her sons out with her for a walk in the hospital park. After the incident with Juleto, they were forbidden from leaving the ward, but I decided to take a chance and let them out. They obediently stood on each side of their mother, and went down the stairs together.

I liked my Sunday shifts. Some of the patients went home, others walked about in the sun and the ward was peaceful. I often used these shifts to get some reading done, and this is what I did that day. I locked myself in the office, opened the window and took out my book. After an hour of reading, my eyes were tired and I leaned out of the window to observe the colours of the yellowing leaves, tending to autumn. The window looked over the hospital backyard. Among the trees, there was all manner of junk – broken tables, discarded old beds, ripped mattresses, rotten slippers, rusted metal plates, cracked porcelain sinks the colour of sea cliffs. Fat cats reigned in this kingdom of oblivion.

I was startled to see people down by the fence. It was the twins and their mother. The mother was extracting food from her bag and carefully arranging it on a broken bedside table. The twins began to stuff their faces with such urgency you'd think they were being hunted down. Their faces went blue from the monumental work of their jaws. The mother continued to extract more and more food. When they had devoured it all, the mother carefully put everything away in her bag. Then she brought out a blanket and spread it out on the ground. The twins sat on it as if by command. The mother remained standing, and slowly began to unbutton her dress. She looked as if she was on the banks of a river, about to go for a swim. Her naked body was astonishingly young and well preserved, like a thirty-year-old woman's. She slowly lay down between her sons. I closed the window quietly, and retreated back into the room.

That evening, the twins were as peaceful as angels. They watched everything there was on TV – the news, the soaps, *The Flintstones*, which they found great fun. At around ten o'clock, the patients started drifting back to their rooms. The twins politely bade me goodnight and went to bed. I returned to the office, opened the window again and looked out into the night. I had seven hours till the end of my shift. This was my last shift as a psychiatric orderly. Next week, I was going to be a university student.

Rider Girl

I KNEW A GIRL ONCE. A RIDER GIRL, IF I MAY SAY SO.

It was a pleasure to watch her undress. She was a mistress of her body. She could do the splits, she could drink a glass of water by lifting it off the floor with her teeth and she could kiss her own heels. But her crowning number was riding a varnished cane.

But I'm getting ahead of myself here.

Sometimes I called her during the day.

'What are you doing?' I asked.

'I'm dancing naked in front of the mirror,' she'd answer.

My head filled with blood but I went on. I went on burning on the pyre of my lust, if I may say so.

'Who is with you today?' I asked my next desperate question.

'Some rich layabout who bought me for the whole day. He

just counted out the notes and they're sitting on my bedside table. Three thousand. I have to work for them, don't I?'

'OK, go and do your work,' I'd say with an effort. 'I'll call you later.'

'Ciao. I'll be waiting,' said my apparition, if I may say so, and hung up.

That's how we chatted.

My job was such that I spent most of my time at home. I had discovered her voice accidentally, during one of my phone orgies. It's just that I liked calling up strange women. Their voices nourished my depleted imagination. After weeks of talking like this on the phone, one day she invited me to the bar where she worked as a stripper. The invitation answered my prayers, and so I accepted at once.

I went early, all dressed up and wearing a cravat and a hanky in my top pocket. My moustache was perfumed and my new shoes showed wine-red reflections. I found a table next to the dance floor and took a look around me. The truth is, I'd been writing porn stories for cheap newspapers and magazines, and in those stories bars grew like mushrooms, resulting in a purely professional contempt for such places.

But this time was different. I sipped a double whisky with lots of ice and waited for my telephone nymph to appear. If she kept me waiting any longer, I'd have a heart attack.

And there it was – the lights were dimmed, drinks were

coming to all the tables, a narrow, lemon-yellow beam of light crept around and she ran out onto the stage.

She was dressed as a rider – in boots, breeches and a jacket. On her splendid head she wore a little jockey's hat with a long peak. For the first five minutes, she rode a varnished cane around the dance floor. She did it so well, I could practically hear the cane neighing from time to time.

Suddenly the little horse came to a halt. My beauty stroked its neck more and more intensely, then jumped off it. She removed her leather belt and it whipped the floor. The jacket flew off. The little silk shirt trembled in an imaginary wind. The music became slower and more dramatic, and the girl's fingers did a little dance up and down the pearl buttons of the shirt.

I took a huge gulp of whisky and my teeth went numb from the ice.

The breeches fell to the floor. The lemon-yellow beam of light fattened and lit her up – she was perfect, like a painting on a stained-glass window with her proud, smooth shoulders, her stomach seemingly crafted by a goldsmith and legs that you could follow day and night like a sleepwalker. She stood naked in her boots and little hat in the middle of the spotlight, until she heard the patrons of the bar yell in ecstasy. Then the little horse neighed, she bestrode it and off she went again. She did a few rounds, and the light and the music followed, then the music stopped. The rider got off the horse and walked among the tables. You could touch her if you wanted to. She seemed to linger by my table, and even seemed to wink at me. My teeth chattered from her naked proximity. Her skin was tender like the membrane on freshly boiled milk, her collar bones rose with her breath in such an exquisite manner that you felt like hanging yourself with ecstasy on the spot. And it would take a composer to describe her spine.

Later, when I was leaving on unsteady legs, I managed to glimpse her one more time. This time she was wearing elegant black leggings and sitting at the bar with two men who looked like arms dealers.

From then on, her bar became my regular place of torment. I went every night, and she paid no attention to me at all. I felt like an idiot: how could I, the author of thousands of frank, unsentimental sex scenes, become infatuated like a schoolboy?

My only consolation was that she continued to be friendly on the phone.

That night I couldn't summon the courage to call her until it became unbearable. But after writing five or six pages of smut, I couldn't bear it any longer, so I picked up the phone and called her.

'Hey, how are you?' I whispered like some spotty teenager, and felt ashamed of my voice.

'I'm resting,' she said. 'I'm not working today. Do you want to come and visit me?' And she gave me her address.

Did I what. This surpassed even my wildest dreams. I ironed my shirt, spent ages choosing a tie and doused myself in cologne, like a barber. Then I was out like a shot. I stopped short of picking lilac in the park.

I took a taxi to the centre of the city. I panted up the stairs to the fourth floor, smoothed my jacket and rang the doorbell.

'Come in, it's open,' the beloved voice said.

I found her lying on a couch, covered up to the chin with a soft camel-hair blanket. A single candle burned in the room.

'Pour yourself a cognac,' she said.

She spoke more slowly than usual, and was audibly nervous.

Then she asked me to play a record. The music threatened to tip me over the edge – I'd never imagined that my beauty could have such melancholy leanings.

'And now blow out the candle,' she said abruptly. I did it without asking questions.

'Come here,' she said in the dark. I found her by feeling my way around. She had thrown off the blanket, and welcomed me into her arms completely naked. Her skin was cool and smelled of nettles.

I don't know how long it lasted, perhaps minutes, perhaps the entire night. At one point I became aware that I was lying on my back and breathing heavily in the darkness. And I realised, with a terrible pang, that the porn stories I'd been writing were unbearably dull and empty.

'Now leave,' I heard her voice. 'And please leave the lights off.'

She was tense, I could feel it. I did as she told me. I got dressed like some automaton, kissed her silken forehead and went into the hallway.

There was a light on here, thank God. In the corner two light aluminium crutches were neatly arranged. At this point I heard steps outside in the stairwell, and someone inserted a key in the lock. I had nowhere to hide.

I remained frozen on the landing.

The door opened, and I found myself face to face with the rider girl.

The Chimpanzee

FRIDAY THE CHIMPANZEE WAS PACING FROM ONE WALL OF the cage to the other. He was a fifteen-year-old male who'd spent his life alone. His black fur shone like melted tar. His bright red penis hung halfway down his thighs, and from time to time Friday would stop walking and rub himself. His face then assumed a pained expression, his eyes glinted strangely and his massive yellow teeth became covered with froth.

At this point, someone unlocked the padlock. It was Tony, Friday's keeper. Tony was a young guy with sand-coloured Bermuda shorts and a pony-tail. There was a girl with him. As always, Tony went inside the tunnel next to the cage and handed Friday a banana, then stroked his balding nape. But unlike other times, the chimpanzee didn't eat his banana. He stayed staring at the frail creature on the other side of the protective glass.

'Madlen,' Tony said to the girl. 'Come over here. He won't do anything.'

'I'm scared,' Madlen said. 'See how he's looking at me.'

She'd just been discharged from her latest stint in the psychiatric unit, and her boyfriend Tony had brought her to the zoo to cheer her up.

The chimp was indeed staring at her without blinking.

'He's a good boy,' Tony said, and kissed his head through the grille.

'He's just like a human being actually,' Madlen said. 'Isn't he sad that he's locked up and alone?'

'No, because he's never known freedom and love. He was born in a zoo and that's been his whole life.'

Madlen went up closer to the cage. With one wary finger, she touched the hairy hand. The chimp didn't react. Then she inserted her whole arm and stroked his back. The hair on the chimp's neck went up.

'Poor thing,' Madlen whispered.

They were about to leave when the chimp started banging on the floor with his hands and throwing himself about the cage.

'Tony, go outside for a moment,' Madlen said suddenly. 'I'll try and calm him down.'

Tony was used to her strange whims. He said he'd be back soon and went out of the pavilion. Madlen touched the chimp again. She slowly slid her hand along his thigh and gripped his member. She pulled him gently towards her. The chimp rose up and glued his stomach to the grille. His penis stuck outside. Madlen started moving her hand up and down. The chimp went dead quiet. Froth dripped on his hairy chest and he gave a low growl. Madlen moved her hand faster and faster. The chimp bellowed, sprayed the cement, then put his big black hands through the grille and took Madlen by the neck.

When Tony came back ten minutes later, they were still locked in an embrace.

He called for help. Someone unlocked the cage and a few men rushed inside. The chimp went crazy and bit a couple of them, then with a big jump he landed next to Madlen. He stood over her fallen body and looked savagely at the heavily breathing men.

They had to shoot him.

One Way Ticket

HE HAD A PROPHET'S BEARD, AN EYE FOR FOUR-LEAF CLOVERS and a hand that always cast the winning dice at backgammon. In winter he went about in his father's old anorak, and in summer he wore the canvas trainers he'd worn for basketball games at high school. We'd shared a desk from Year One to Year Eleven. We called each other Joe, as in that children's song about Lemonade Joe: 'Joe peeks from the grave, winks with his left eye…' or however it went.

'So, are we leaving, Joe?' he asked.

I looked at his eyes, wide-set like a falcon's, and decided to be honest.

'I can't, Joe. I can't leave my wife behind, and the little ones.'

'You know what's best. It's just that staying here is a joke.

Over there, the weekly dole comes to the same as the Bulgarian president's monthly salary.'

'I know, Joe,' I said. 'But I can't.'

'It would've been cool to be in this together. Like before, Joe,' my friend said. 'To take our first steps in America together. It's so much better to have someone prompting from the back desk.'

Over the next few days we spoke by phone. He told me his dates. At the appointed hour I was at the airport, in the grubby hall where people said their farewells and where they still sold souvenirs made at the time when Precious Wilson sang 'One Way Ticket'.

Soon Joe was there too, wearing his old anorak and, for some reason, the old canvas trainers – despite the snow outside. We smoked a fag, he said to kiss my wife and the kiddies from Uncle Joe, then he slung his sports bag over his shoulder, winked at me, took a sip from the hip flask in his pocket and gave me a drink too, and then he went to that passenger door through which they were all going, and he disappeared.

I went outside to wait for the bus back into town, but there was no bus, so eventually I was forced to walk. The snow creaked under my feet. A broad-spectrum Bulgarian silence lay over the snowy wasteland, and only the engine roar of the odd departing plane ripped through it.

Something stumbled into my legs. When I bent down, I saw a rabbit with bleeding feet. He was looking straight into my eyes, and his entire body shook from his beating heart. I stroked his ears and he came hopping after me in an odd way. After a hundred steps or so I saw something black on the snow. The rabbit's hackles went up. It was a dog, curled up into a ball. When I approached, he whimpered and licked my hand. I stroked his head and together, the three of us carried on. Soon, a bird ran into me and fell on the snow. It was a raven. I picked it up carefully, unzipped my jacket and put it next to my chest.

With each step we took, the cold got worse. The field around us looked like a giant iceberg. We struggled on, until I had to stop and with an enormous effort of will I started scraping the icy snow together and making it into a pile. When the pile was high enough, I dug inside it to make something resembling an igloo. We all went inside the igloo and huddled together. The raven had come to its senses and was now sitting on my shoulder and warming my cheek pleasantly.

'So long, Joe,' I said. 'And don't forget to write or call to let me know what's up with that tasty Precious Wilson. Has she shrivelled up yet, or what?'

And with my left eye I winked at Joe, high up in the sky.

Django

ALONG THE STONE RAILING OF THE TRAIN-LINE BRIDGE, huge rusted letters said: LONG LIVE LENIN'S DEEDS! Under the bridge lived a Gypsy family. The woman had still beautiful shoulders and feverish eyes. She wore patched quilted trousers and men's shoes with their backs squashed down, like slippers. Her name was Kera.

The man was brown and dry like a leather strap. In his beard, flashes of white were already starting to show. Every morning, he put an old belt around his coat, flopped a heavy coil of hemp rope over his shoulder, waited for the seven thirty passenger train which slowed down as it passed over the bridge and jumped on the last carriage. He worked as a labourer in Sofia for small change. His name was Meto.

Kera and Meto had three children. The oldest was ten-year-old Django. He was already quite tall and had the right build for a labourer. But he didn't care much for work. Django spent the days squatting by the railway line, blowing a reed whistle. The girls were three and five. They each had a piece of gauze hanging on strings around their necks, with damp bread inside. When they were hungry, they'd suck on the bread. The girls had no names.

The bridge sheltered them, and it was really quite liveable down here. With a few rugs and a few sticks, Meto had built them a hut. Kera had found a discarded pot that was in pretty good nick, and it was her pride and joy. In the morning, after seeing Meto off, she took the girls with her to the nearest railway station of Rebrovo, about three kilometres from their bridge. There, she swept the station café and sometimes managed to palm-read for some woman, or get a bit of white bread or clothes for the girls.

In the evening, the family gathered under the bridge. When Meto had made a bit of money, the fire under the bridge played like a monkey, and there was soup bubbling in the pot. With each sip of rakia from his grubby, chewed-up cup, Meto's voice fluttered higher and higher, as if it had wings. Then the kids fell asleep, and Meto would sing his long, even-keeled song without words, just like the train's wheels. If he wasn't dead drunk, in the dim light of the dying fire he would remember Kera and look inside her eyes, black like a nymph's. Sometimes Kera looked back, and pulled him away from the light of the fire and took him in her arms.

When there was no money to bring back, the flames of the fire cast shadows against the walls of the bridge like mean dogs. Meto stared hard at some invisible point and the kids hid under the rugs. Then Kera would get up, pull off her trousers hardened with grime, and go wash in the river. With reptilian movements she'd pull on a stolen tight skirt, take out a little mirror and a lipstick and paint her mouth in the shape of a heart. Then she took off, up to the motorway where the night trucks passed.

One evening, Meto didn't return. Django kept trying to light a fire, but a cold wind had risen in the gorge and kept putting out the flame. In the morning, dizzy with tiredness, Django went walking by the railway line to look for his father. He returned at dusk, bent low under the weight of his father's hemp rope. In his hand, he gripped the canister in which his father carried his rakia during the day.

'Open it,' he said to his mother.

Kera unscrewed the cap.

'Pour me some,' Django said.

Kera poured some in Meto's chewed-up cup. Django poured off a bit onto the earth, then poured the rest into his throat and doubled up with pain.

His mother started wailing. She wailed and took off her

trousers, wailed and put on the skirt, wailed and smeared lip-stick over her face.

Django was sitting in his father's usual spot.

'You're staying here,' he said to his mother. 'You're not going anywhere.'

Kera sat back on the stones and continued wailing. She wailed all night, like a wolf.

In the morning, Django took out his father's razor and scraped his face. His tender skin flared up, but he gritted his teeth. He put a rope around his waist, picked up his dad's old knife and put it in his pocket. Then he climbed up onto the bridge to wait for the passenger train at seven-thirty. When it came, he jumped on the last carriage. Gripping the cold iron, Django travelled towards Sofia. In a few minutes, the train thundered over a ravine. Ravens hovered overhead, and Django's face went stone-grey. He felt in his pocket for his treasures: the reed whistle and the knife. And he squinted against the heavy, bitter, ash-laden wind that was coming his way.

Lucky Hit

CHRISTOPHOR K.'S TROUBLES STARTED IN THE MORNing. First, he had to take inventories into the accounting department, but those stupid cows with purple nails and shaved shanks told him to do the accounting himself, because they were up to here with work. Then he discovered that the inventories were a complete mess, as if Satan himself had been at work, and just when he had finished the accounting – thank God it was over! – just then someone rushed in with two urgent letters to be signed by Comrade Somov himself, so Christophor K. ran to his office with sweet thoughts of little Illina who'd greet him there, but Comrade Somov wasn't there, so Christophor K. sat down to wait for him. He was waiting so diligently, with eyes so downcast with patience, that little Illina finally took pity on him and made him a real Nescafé, with a thick frothy top.

Christophor K. drank his coffee and waited some more, but Comrade Somov still didn't come and Christophor K. became anxious because each letter had four red exclamation marks for urgency, and he started sweating with anxiety, an old problem of his, resulting in two big stains under his arms, he just knew it, and he knew it was unacceptable to present oneself to Comrade Somov in this condition, sweating like a pig. Thank God he had the presence of mind to use Comrade Somov's absence to dash off to the bathroom and take the terrifying risk of being found like this, shirtless and down to his white singlet, washing his armpits with soap and then splashing himself with cold water and spluttering like a horse, keeping an eye on the door. Thank God nothing happened, and he managed to dry himself in the end. In the corridor, he ran into Pesho and was hugely relieved to see his colleague because Pesho was the most cunning fox here in Glavprom, and he was sure to know the whereabouts of Comrade Somov so Christophor K. quickly asked him whether Comrade Somov had been seen today, and Pesho ruffled his cunning sideburns and said that a car was leaving any moment now for the site where Comrade Somov was, so don't mess about, Pesho said, but go and ask if you can catch a ride. Christophor K. galloped down the corridor and explained to the travel party how important it was to find Comrade Somov and fortunately, they turned out to be decent folk and put him in the back of the truck because there was no room in the front.

The trip was long, and the truck kept stopping and starting, climbing and descending, and in the covered back, Christophor K. crouched among oily rags, spades, cases and tubes and wondered why on earth he hadn't had breakfast this morning, thanks to which his stomach was now rumbling, on top of everything else today.

Finally, the truck came to a halt. A field stretched away on all sides, all dug up and strewn with pipes and iron scrap. About fifty metres into the field, a few men stood around an excavation site. Christophor K. headed towards them, stepping over the cables and climbing over the pipes and mounds of earth. The men were intently studying a drawing spread out before them. Christophor K. asked the nearest person who Comrade Somov was, but the man just shushed him and Christophor K. didn't insist. After a while, he felt icy trickles of sweat run down his back and the rumblings of a distant toothache, and he asked after Comrade Somov again. The man turned round and looked him up and down, a smoked-down fag sparkling in the corner of his mouth. Then he spat out the fag and nodded towards the centre of the gathering. Christophor K. moved his feet and swallowed dryly. Then he relished again the approaching toothache and savoured the storm, the leaden sky in his head, the thunder that would split him in half, the nests fallen on the ground, the branches that twist and cut down everything in sight like sabres. Suddenly, the backs of the men closed in before him like a wall, and after a short while, Christophor K. left.

He wandered across the field for a long time. He jumped over pits and more piles of earth, crawled, lizard-like, inside cement pipes, walked around bulldozers and abandoned carriages, splashed across small, crusty ponds hung with clusters of frogs, and finally reached the motorway. Nobody pulled over, and Christophor K. despaired, and in his despair he started cursing every passing car, in fact he felt like pelting them with lumps of earth, at least there was no shortage of those, and to prevent himself from doing just that, he shoved his hands into his pockets and slowly walked along the motorway. The squeal of brakes took him by surprise. The car that had pulled over was rather strange – it was like a jeep but bigger, and armoured on both sides with thick grilles, which must be the kind of vehicles used in the African savannah for hunting large felines, or at least that's what Christophor K. thought. The driver was about fifty and in an excellent mood, so soon Christophor K. started feeling fine himself, and all his bitterness evaporated, in fact he even started humming a little tune, an old school tune to which he'd forgotten the words.

The jeep flew along the motorway, straight towards the blood-red sky, overtaking all the other cars and shaking and howling with joy. Christophor K. managed to take a peek at the driver, and the first thing he noticed were his thick wrists and also the tattoos of sirens, masculine oaths and all manner of numbers among the hairs of his forearms. His head was gnawed by scars and bumps, his neck was cut by lines like a ravine by streams, and his shoulder exuded such raw animal strength that Christophor K. choked on his tune and tried to start a conversation. The driver was laughing a lot, and his ha-ha-ha-ha thundered inside the car and drowned out the roar of the engine. At one point, as Christophor K. was telling him about the elusive Comrade Somov, the driver let go of the steering wheel and lit a cigarette, and rippled with waves of mirth. Then he said that he'd give a bag of gold if only he could meet that Comrade Somov and show him who was boss. Christophor K. timidly asked where he would find that much gold, and the driver confided in him that gold wasn't a problem for him. In whispers, he told the now very worried Christophor K. that he was a bounty-hunter and had been all his life, and always would be. In Bulgaria, the driver whispered, there was so much buried gold that a single human life was not enough to dig it all out. Just the treasure of Tsar Ivan Shishman, the last medieval Bulgarian king, would be enough to tide him over. Christophor K. nodded in agreement and also to show how interested he was, but deep down he was thanking the heavens that they were now approaching the city. He'd make it just in time to call in at the office and explain that he hadn't got hold of Comrade Somov, and, casually, to ask out the delicate, wafer-like little Illina – yes, ask out Illina of the thick eyelashes and butterfly soul. The thought of little Illina restored some of his confidence.

The car was now flying over the wrecked tarmac of the city outskirts, past whitewashed houses and pretty gardens with quince trees bright like lit candles, past miraculously preserved high stone wells pointing at the sky like fingers, and Christophor K. noticed that it was strangely quiet around here, there were no women, children or old men, it was all deadly quiet, and even the leaves on the tree branches didn't move. However, soon they approached a gathering of people near some trees, and while Christophor K. was trying to work out what was going on, the car veered down a rough road, shook over the unpaved earth and pulled up right next to the small crowd.

The driver mumbled something about stretching their legs and invited Christophor K. to get out, then erupted from his seat. They found themselves right in the middle of it all. People in different coloured paper hats were moving in seemingly pointless concentric circles, some were eating sandwiches, others were smoking, and the further they went into the crowd, the stranger it all became, and now people were wearing long hemp shirts with string around the waist, and chain mail, and there was the odd helmeted man. The driver seemed in his element here: he walked about and inspected the scene at his leisure. And suddenly, among the buzz of voices, they heard weeping, which at first seemed to come from the earth, but soon it got nearer and filled the sky, and just then Christophor K. saw a human pile-up of weeping men, and their weeping broke his heart and misted his eyes. What's going on here? asked his companion in a loud voice, and an old man appeared as if out of nowhere and explained that this was the army of Tsar Ivan Shishman. The old man was plastered and lurched this way and that, but when he pulled at their sleeves, they followed him. Are you heroes, by any chance, the old man asked them, because if you are, there's a big sword made of pure steel over there which nobody can pull out, it's very heavy and very sharp, and if you are heroes, go and give it a try. Then the old man started weeping too, and pointed at the place where the sword was sticking out of the ground. Christophor K. touched the handle gingerly – its silver was antique and beautifully crafted. His powerful companion laughed, stood over the sword and took hold of it. The tendons of his neck strained, his eyes went blood-red, black sweat poured from his forehead and then the earth shook, the metal rang and the sword was out before their eyes. Its beautiful blue steel gladdened Christophor K.'s soul. Lead us onwards, big hero, the old man said, stumbling behind them, but the big hero was already marching away, dragging Christophor K. by the hand and before he knew what was happening, they were inside the car and out of there. No way, guffawed the driver, no way are we going to fall into the hands of these silly movie folk.

By the time Christophor K. came to his senses, they were moving among endless rows of tower blocks, petrol stations and supermarkets. There were tons of people everywhere, and only the odd dusty whirlwind out in the sparse potato fields changed the view. From here Christophor K. could get back by public transport, but he didn't have the guts to speak out. The car was now making its way into the city centre, and through the mud-spattered front windscreen he could see the shadows of moving people, the thick flow of cars, the enraged trams coming their way. The speed of it all was terrifying, so Christophor K. decided to act now and cleared his throat and thanked the driver for the ride, and asked him to stop wherever he could. Just as he thought the driver hadn't heard him, they slowed down and turned into a quiet side-street with chestnut trees. The driver pulled over and turned to Christophor K. with a huge smile, and just as Christophor K. started thanking him again, the man, still luminously smiling, reached over and yanked his jaw open with his vicelike fingers and took a good look at his mouth. Aha, the driver jumped with joy, he hadn't been wrong about this, and with a sudden movement, as if with pliers, he pulled out Christophor K.'s gold tooth. Christophor K. hardly felt any pain, he hardly felt anything at all, and as he walked towards the office to hand in the two ill-fated letters, he felt with the tip of his tongue the little bloody hole where his tooth had been. He'd become used to the sour taste of gold.

It was only at the entrance of the office building that he realised he didn't have the letters. He must have left them behind in the car. It was pointless to go upstairs to the office, so the only thing he could think of was to call little Illina. She couldn't remember him straight away, but when he reminded her of the morning coffee, she agreed to see him for an hour or two, no more. Christophor K. snapped into action and bought bread, salami and wine, and walked home without hurrying.

It must have been the late afternoon hour that explained the deserted streets at the last tram stop where his rendezvous with little Illina was. While he waited for her, Christophor K. noticed a mound on the street which he hadn't seen before. He approached carefully and saw that it was a horse lying sideways. In the dusk, the horse looked enormous, like a hill, and its flank gleamed with a dreadful force, as if it was about to rise up and look at him with surprised violet eyes and gallop away. It was only after Christophor K. had walked around the horse that he was reassured it was truly dead – the wounds on the horse's back were clearly visible, and so was the froth of agony on its mouth and the frost over the beautiful eyes. Christophor K. withdrew into the shadow of an awning.

He drank a lot that night, and little Illina got tipsy too, and after a brief ladylike hesitation, she offered him her freckled little body. Christophor K. crunched it up at once and then fell into such a state of bliss that he even stopped feeling the little hole and soon enough, it felt as if there had never been a tooth there at all, as if he'd been born with this little hole in his mouth.

In the morning, he woke up feeling fresh and sure of himself, shaved with care and saw little Illina off on the staircase of Glavprom. His colleagues greeted him with much adoring silence and soon, he heard that Somov had personally called to thank Christophor K. for his excellent work and to express his astonishment at the quick delivery of the two very urgent letters, and at this point his colleagues started moving their upper lips quickly, like rabbits, and in confidential whispers they passed down to him Somov's last words, which was to say that Somov was sending Christophor K. his exclusive, personal greetings.

The Eagle

THE PICK-UP TRUCK STOPPED IN FRONT OF THE TOWER BLOCK. The kids surrounded it. 'Eagle! Eagle!' they screamed. A dozen men, hot from drinking, rushed out of their watering hole in a basement. The kids shook all over, as if struck by an electric shock.

Orlin's father came heavily out of the truck. His unblinking eyes swept triumphantly over the brown wasteland beyond the block and the distant motorway, he smoothed his raven hair, spat on the wrecked pavement and looked inside the back of the truck. Orlin came over from the crowd of kids and stood by his father. He was standing on tiptoes, to look taller. Orlin meant Eagle.

The drinking men tossed away their fags, lit more cigarettes and came to the truck. In the back, there was an eagle. It was

174

tied up with rope and its enormous wings filled the entire space. Its head was bloodied, and he'd made bullet-like holes in the tin with his beak. Orlin's father lit up a cigarette, coughed and started telling the story.

It was dusk. The windows in the nearby blocks of flats lit up. The distant motorway turned into a flaming ribbon of Morse-code messages. The men got to work. Six of the biggest guys lifted up the eagle and carried him up the stairs of the building. The tremendous bird didn't resist. Only once, on the landing before the last, one of the carriers pulled his wing too hard, and the eagle reached for him with its claws. The man fell back down the stairs, four bloody grooves across his face. His wild cry haunted the stairwell with its echo.

They just about broke their backs trying to haul the eagle up onto the asphalt roof of the tower block. Up there, a forest of aerials stretched out on all sides and vibrated in the wind with an eerie ring. Someone brought more rope, and they tied the eagle even more tightly. They wound the ends of the ropes around two big iron rings fixed into the cement. Then it was party time. Everyone congratulated Orlin's father, patting him on the back.

Soon, the roof became chock-a-block with people. Some were holding torches, which they waved about. The kids screamed themselves raw.

Suddenly, Orlin's mother appeared, forging a path through

the crowd. She was holding a clay dish full of water. She put the dish in front of the eagle, smoothed her hair behind her ear, kneeled down and watched him drink.

The School-leaver

BEFORE WE KNEW IT, KALINA BECAME A SCHOOL-LEAVER. It was only yesterday that a little girl with scraped knees was running down the street, coming into the house yards and picking cherries from our trees. Then, suddenly, the little girl grew up and turned into something resembling a freckled doe with disproportionately long limbs and enormous eyes. As soon as she returned from school, Kalina would go and play with Yonko's lambs, help Lazar the sculptor to wet his clay, buy bread and milk for the old fiddle-player Stanoiko, and walk Filip's dog, which had taken to howling for entire days ever since Filip's wife and kids went to America and Filip turned to drinking. She bought a turtle for my little ones, and taught my daughter to weave wreaths from willow branches and my son to shoot with a slingshot. She was the only one brave enough to talk to the gangster Rony Manchev-Baltya, in the last house at the end of the street, when he returned in the early mornings with eyes like holes in the snow.

At the start of this year, we discovered a girl that was Kalina and yet wasn't her. All I can say is this: when the truck drivers transporting logs for the palace being built at the top of the hill and belonging to some sheikh saw Kalina, they would brake, pull over in the ditch and light up a cigarette with trembling hands.

It was the end of May – the time for the school prom. The whole street got together to see Kalina off to the prom. Her parents brought out chairs and benches in the courtyard but there were so many guests, we had to sit on the grass. Yonko had roasted a lamb. Filip brought the wine. Lazar the sculptor sang a few songs with his thick, priestly voice. Old Stanoiko played on his fiddle with his fingers – the bow had been broken half a century ago. I read out my new ode. Kalina walked among us in jeans and a t-shirt until the last minute, but when she came out in her ball gown, even the wind went quiet and lay at her feet like a dog.

People started whispering. Rony Manchev-Baltya was here, hugging a big bunch of red roses. He handed them to her and stepped aside. Close up, his eyes were as soft as velvet.

Now we were all waiting for Kalina's escort, and we were dying of curiosity. Rony casually adjusted the gun under his jacket. It started getting dark. Finally, a silver limousine glided by the fence. It was so long, we twisted our necks trying to see all of it. The tinted window of the left-hand door slid down and the sheikh signalled to Kalina to get in.

Galileo

THE NIGHT HAD GONE PEACEFULLY IN THE PSYCHIATRIC hospital of Kurilo. Now, in the early morning, the massive hospital park smelled of fresh wet soil. In the tree branches, nightingales sang like there was no tomorrow. Pink, shiny worms lay along the rain-polished main alley like giant question marks. Galileo walked carefully around them. He had tied his rusty hospital gown at the waist with wire. Mornings always inspired him. The best part of the day was coming up – buying coffee and cigarettes from the kiosk at the hospital gates. Then he'd crouch by the telegraph pole, sip his coffee and chain-smoke. Tobacco stimulated his thoughts and after a difficult, oblivious night wiped out by medication, he'd be able once again to reflect on worldly matters.

The kiosk, however, was still closed. Galileo looked around

helplessly. Despair came over him suddenly like a truckload of gravel. And now, from out of the guard's kiosk came Gregor the Sphinx. The Sphinx always had cigarettes, and no matter how much Galileo hated him, he begged him for one.

'Only if you say "I'm a piece of shit"!' the Sphinx mooed.

'I'm a piece of shit.'

'OK,' the Sphinx said. He brought out a crumpled packet of cigarettes from the pocket of his khaki jacket, shook out a single cigarette and handed it to Galileo. Galileo lit up with shaky hands and when he drew the first lungful of smoke, he heard the nightingales once again.

'What's the latest on the war?' he asked, stammering with emotion.

'The war?' the Sphinx looked at him curiously and his cheeks folded up like corrugated iron. 'The war is over.'

Galileo dropped his cigarette, looked around in panic and ran back to the hospital. The Sphinx shook with laughter.

'The war is over!' Galileo screamed. He flew into the dormitories and started shaking the other patients awake. He pulled off their blankets, tugged at their pillows, heavy like bags of cement, opened the windows. 'The war is over!'

In the doorway Panteley the orderly appeared, big and heavy like a mammoth.

'You motherfucking motherfucker,' he growled in his sleepy bass, and with one hand he effortlessly pinned Galileo to the iron frame of his bed. With the other he started to tie him down with the straps – first his arms, then his legs. 'People are still sleeping, you motherfucking motherfucker.'

The Cricket

THE HEAD DOCTOR OF THE KURILO PSYCHIATRIC HOSPITAL, Dr Delibaltov, summoned Mad Max to his office and solemnly handed him five kilograms of paperwork. Here was twenty years of Max's case history: the illness, the tests, the diagnoses.

'Sit down, don't just stand there,' he invited Mad Max.

Mad Max perched gently on the cracked edge of the black vinyl couch. Dr Delibaltov sat behind his desk, looked around and produced a bottle of cognac. This was a historic moment, and he could allow himself a small indulgence in the circumstances – a little drink in the presence of a patient. But this wasn't just any patient – this was Mad Max, Kurilo's mascot. And today, they had to say goodbye. That's why the doctor had called Mad Max in today – to part with dignity, like normal people.

'We're the veterans here, you and I. True, we're on different sides of the divide, but I think we've both behaved like real men. That's why I'll be honest with you.'

Dr Delibaltov licked his lips, then quickly poured himself another glass, glanced around and swallowed it quickly, as if someone was about to slap his hand in reprimand.

'To cut a long story short,' he looked Mad Max in the eyes, 'I called you in because it's time to say goodbye. I didn't expect this, and you probably didn't either, but that's life, full of surprises. Your stay with us has come to an end.'

Mad Max kept nodding and smiling.

'That's it, my friend. In this country, there is no more money for institutions like ours. So, as of today, you are a free man.'

Dr Delibaltov got up. Mad Max also jumped to his feet. He had a vague, distant expression on his face, as if all this wasn't happening to him. He exited through the door backwards, clutching the pile of paperwork and bowing ceremonially to Dr Delibaltov. When the door closed, the doctor stood by the window and lit a cigarette. He had to record this moment, the moment when Mad Max went out through the hospital gates. Twenty years of that man's life had passed here, in the grey rooms and rusty alleys of the hospital park.

A few moments later, Dr Delibaltov saw Mad Max downstairs. He was dressed in civilian clothes – a shockingly old-fashioned alpaca jacket with sleeves that were too short for him, chequered trousers that made him look like a clown and some grubby canvas shoes. He had no luggage. He'd probably left behind in room number six the five kilos of paperwork which described in great detail just how hopelessly insane he was.

Mad Max became smaller and smaller, until he vanished at the end of the main alley. Dr Delibaltov removed his glasses, rubbed his inflamed eyes with the back of his hand and once again sat down heavily at his desk. He had some hard work ahead of him. He had to decide who else to discharge.

Meanwhile, Mad Max was walking down the road towards the centre of the town. Everything was interesting to him, especially the fact that the hospital gates were behind him. An old woman was coming his way. For some reason, she looked like an ox, perhaps because she was big and dressed in black. Mad Max wished she could laugh, he wished her sorrowful white face could turn happy. Perhaps she even had dimples in her cheeks when she smiled. He straightened up and started marching with stiff legs, lifting them high up. But the old woman didn't smile, far from it. She froze up, looked at him with worry, crossed herself and hurried along. Mad Max cursed her cheerfully with his fingers and continued along the wrecked tarmac, carefully avoiding the potholes.

On his right-hand side, abandoned factory buildings appeared. Someone had oil-painted large letters on a wall facing the road: 'Freedom or Death!!!' Mad Max went up to the graffiti and touched the letters. They were large and rough like ox tongues, and made him feel that the wall had been built especially to accommodate these letters. Mad Max crouched, leaned against the wall and had a cigarette. This is what they did in the hospital bathrooms: they'd crouch by the wall and smoke in silence.

A truck was coming his way, an old blue truck. Mad Max carefully trampled his cigarette underfoot, got up and waved. The driver went past him but then suddenly braked, backed up and stopped right beside him in a cloud of dust. When Mad Max got in, the small driver stepped on it with gusto. He was a very young guy with a quicklime-stained beanie pulled down to his eyes.

'Hi,' said Mad Max. 'I'm Mad Max. And what's your name?'

'My name's Mad Ventsi,' said the driver. 'Where are you going?'

'Wherever.'

'OK, then we're in it together. I left my fucking job and I'm off to a protest in Sofia. Those motherfuckers. The whole country's up against them, on strike, and those bastards aren't even moving their fat arses. And my fucking boss is brown-nosing them. You're not going anywhere, he goes, you're staying right here in the quarry and getting on with it. I go, Fuck you, and I got in the truck and went without asking permission from anybody. 'Cause if I don't go, if you don't go, if what's-his-name doesn't go, we'll stay in the shit. No one will know we've had it. Right?'

'Right,' Mad Max agreed.

They were speeding along the motorway now, going at a

hundred and twenty kilometres per hour right over the white line. The policeman at the next crossroads only had time to blink as they flashed past him.

'Under your seat there's a flag,' Ventsi said. 'Stick it out the window. Fuck it. We got to show who we are and what we're fighting for.'

Mad Max pulled out the wooden handle, unwound the fabric, wound down the window and stuck the flag out. It flapped violently in the wind.

Ventsi entered Sofia via the outer suburb of Lyulin. A few brothers and sisters of the struggle were walking in single file across the muddy fields of the Roma slums at Filipovtsi. When they saw the speeding truck, at first they froze up out of habit, like icon thieves caught red-handed by the padre, but then they started jumping up and down, waving their arms. The pavements were full of people, alone or in groups, and many of the children were carrying little flags. Ventsi enjoyed the sight of them from his driver's cabin, and kept beeping the horn, which produced the deafening sound of a wounded elephant. People smiled and greeted the truck with their little flags or with the sign of V for victory.

'See, see, I told you!' Ventsi wriggled in his seat. 'We'll blow those arseholes away like dry turds.'

A group of teenagers, their shoulders covered with large tri-colour flags waved at them. Ventsi braked with force. The boys and girls climbed up into the open bodywork and banged on the roof of the cabin to say they were ready to go. Ventsi stepped on it like there was no tomorrow.

The closer they came to the centre of the city, the harder it was to get through. The streets were clogged with people. Ventsi took Slivnitsa Boulevard, turned down Hristo Botev and reached Macedonia Square before he gave up.

'This is us,' he said, jumped down, banged the door and left the truck to its own devices. Soon, he disappeared into the crowd. Mad Max also got off, clutching the flag tight with both hands. The crowd swallowed him up at once, propped him up with their shoulders and pulled him along. Their faces had a grim cheer about them. Mad Max was searching for Ventsi, but couldn't see him anywhere. The teenage hitchhikers were gone too. The procession crept slowly along the boulevard. Mad Max walked along with the rest, waving the flag up high. Suddenly, he was desperate for a smoke, but there were no walls to crouch by anywhere in sight. At the Five Corners, the human river took a left turn down Patriarch Evtimyi Avenue. A boy and a girl were walking next to Mad Max. They were very young, no more than sixteen, and their shoulder-length hair was bound in ribbons. They used every halt in the crowd's movement to kiss. They had wrapped themselves in a large flag and looked like a strange and gorgeous two-headed creature.

The thick stream of people was moving with excruciating

slowness, but after half an hour, the head end of the procession reached the Pope's Corner. Mad Max had managed to edge ahead, and was now in the second or third row. The two-headed creature kept up the pace too, and they even managed to introduce themselves to him. The boy was Janny, and the girl Jenny. At the Pope's Corner, the front of the procession halted. The crossroads ahead was blocked by a cordon of heavily armed policemen. They wore helmets and shields, and many of them were chewing gum. Mad Max stood there for a quarter of an hour, like everyone else, then suddenly he got fed up. He'd liked being carried along by all these people.

Mad Max forged himself a path ahead and got to the open space between the first row of protesters and the police. He didn't have a plan, he just knew that he didn't want to be stuck in one place. Then he remembered how he'd scared the old woman on the road, and straightened up his body. With his arms next to his trunk and stiff legs, he marched towards the policemen. Laughter rose from the ranks of the protesters and soon spread until it became unstoppable. The wave of laughter caught on even among those further back who couldn't see. This encouraged Mad Max, and he carried on marching in this way along the cordon of policemen, causing storms of laughter. One of the policemen stepped forward, lifted his baton like a sabre and cut Mad Max down. After the third blow, Mad Max fell to the ground. The policeman continued to beat him and was joined by another. Mad Max stopped seeing and hearing. He lay on the tarmac and twitched. At one point he felt himself being dragged somewhere. He felt support behind his back. When he started hearing and seeing again, he realised that he'd been propped up against a wall. He remembered that he felt like smoking and pushed a cigarette into his mouth. He lit up, but when he inhaled, a ghastly pain cut across him and he tasted blood in his mouth. He swallowed it down and looked around. It was night and he was on the pavement next to some building. The street lamps and lit-up shop signs were reflected on the wet grainy asphalt of the empty streets, and somewhere in the distance he heard the savage roar of a thousand human throats.

Mad Max tried to remember the beginning of this strange day, and vaguely recalled the red eyes of Dr Delibaltov, the rusty alley, the clapped-out truck, and then it went blank. And anyway, all this seemed so confused and distant, as if he'd lived it in some other life, so he stopped thinking about it. Now he was overcome by another thought which became more and more urgent and anxious. He realised that in the morning, he'd forgotten to feed his pet cricket who lived in a shoe box under his bed in room number six. The cricket was going to starve to death without him. His anxiety became intolerable. Mad Max swallowed the blood in his mouth, and across the enormous distance he'd travelled that day, with wide-open eyes, he turned his gaze towards his beloved, his one and only cricket.

The Portrait

ZURA SELLS VEGETABLES AT THE MARKET – POTATOES, THAT sort of thing. She and Murray got themselves a stall three months ago. Murray doesn't drink so much now 'cause they have to work. Well, he still hits the *mastika* but only at night, when they go home.

The thing is, he's just too cool to work, so he turns up at the market around lunchtime. By which time Zura has worked her arse off. First thing in the morning, she goes down to the cellar where they keep their veg, and she loads the plastic bags onto the cart. Then she pushes the effing cart across town all the way to the bloody market. She sets up the stall, sprays the veg with water to freshen it up, and drinks a strong coffee if she has the time with her stall neighbour Victor, the guy who acts like he's a painter and keeps having her on about doing her portrait naked, with just a red scarf around the waist.

Zura pushes the heavy effing cart along the road, and the effing drivers keep beeping their horns something chronic. And lately, there's this blond moron who drives slowly right behind her, and when Zura turns round he sends her kisses. He's got a hell of a car and a white shirt and bright tie every morning, no joke, like he's just taken off the wrapping paper or something.

Last night, though, Murray drank like a pig. His brother-in-law came over and that was that – they drank like the bloody Gypsies they were. So today Zura's really angry 'cause she has to work her arse off again. She pushes the cart and bites her lips. And the moron in the car is there again, right behind her, fresh and smiley like a melon. Not just that, but this time he actually comes all the way to the market, and he gets out of the car and he goes: Want to come with me for an hour? And he shows her some dollars or something in his pocket. Zura got angry at first, 'cause she ain't nobody's slut, but then she said to herself, I'll show that motherfucker layabout Murray, he can go stick it, so she told the blond one to wait, she took her cart to her stall, asked Victor to keep an eye on her produce 'cause she had to sort something out, she'll be right back, then she ran to the blond one and jumped in his car.

She came back in the midday heat, quickly set her veg up, sprayed it, sat on an upturned case and said to Victor, What about a strong coffee? But there was something the matter with

Victor, 'cause he was all quiet. Zura tried teasing him and said, Hey, what about that portrait, the one where I'm naked with just a red scarf round my waist? And Victor's all quiet, then suddenly he goes, 'What're you bloody on about?'

The Dragon

BOZHANA LIVED UP ON THE HILLSIDE, BUT EVEN SO THE path to her house was like a high street. The branches of the linden tree by the gate were snapped, the little stone fence was worn down by lads' elbows, her little garden trodden and full of fags. When the old men outside the village pub saw her coming down with her tin water jugs balancing on a wooden pole over her shoulder, as was the custom, they poured the rakia straight down their throats and their eyes took on a special sheen. And so it went from day to day. Time passed, the lads who'd trodden her garden down got married, the old men in the pub died out, and when thick snow fell over the village, Bozhana knew that she was an old maid.

Nobody came for her any more. Her dad, the one with the crushed leg after a beech tree fell on it three years back, would say to her: 'Bozhana, Bozhana, I told you to cover your head and not to give your flowers away and not to come back with empty jugs, but you didn't listen. Now you're as lonely as a cuckoo. Go and mend the clothes in your dowry before the moths eat it all.'

One morning, Bozhana had just lit up the stove in the sitting room and was outside throwing out the ashes, when a big horse cart stopped outside the gate. The two horses had froth on their mouths, and when they snorted to a halt, their hot breath melted the snow. A man of a certain age jumped down, though he was still in his prime, strong and powerful. He looked her up and down.

'Come, fair maiden, let's go in, I have something to discuss with your dad.'

And without further ado, he went into the house.

Her dad was glad to have guests. He propped himself up in his invalid's bed, called for her to pour some rakia and after the second drink, he got all red-faced and merry. Bozhana pottered about and went out to feed the hens, and when she came back, she heard her father say 'son-in-law' to the guest, and pat him on the shoulder.

'Sit down,' he gestured to her. 'This good man has come from the fields to look for a bride. I say, there's no better homemaker than you. Next Sunday we'll have the wedding, and that's that. Your mother will rest in her grave then.'

The stranger rose and his head hit the ceiling. He pinched

Bozhana on the neck, ran back to his cart and jumped up on his seat. Fire came out of the horses' nostrils, and soon there was nothing left of them, only black stones.

Bozhana leaned her face on her dad's shoulder.

'Don't give me to him, Daddy,' she wept, 'don't give me to him. Did you see his hands, Daddy, all covered in snake scales!'

'You heard what I said,' her father said. 'The wedding is on Sunday. Go and wash the rugs, guests are coming to the house.'

The Orphan

MARIN THE ORPHAN IS DESPERATE TO GET MARRIED. BUT he's as poor as a church mouse, so poor he can't afford to shave, let alone get married.

Otherwise, he's chosen his bride-to-be – the priest's daughter Tsonka. She is like a teardrop with her arched brows, her ankles thin as spindles, her bosoms like freshly risen dough.

One day Marin got fed up with being poor and sat down to hatch a plan. He was thinking so hard his head started smoking like a pot forgotten in a hot oven. Marin ran to the well and poured a bucket of water over his head, then sat down to think again. By midnight, he hadn't come up with anything so he went to bed. He slept and he dreamed that in a corner of his house, his great-grandfather, Slavei the brigand, had buried some treasure. A whole pot of gold coins.

Marin leaped out of bed before dawn. He poured a bucket of water over his head and picked up the spade. By lunchtime he'd dug out the corner so much, his house squatted onto one side. The village folk came to watch Marin pull his house down. The men clicked their tongues, the women crossed themselves. When Marin took a break at noon, they asked him why he was pulling his house down. "Cause there's gold underneath,' Marin said. 'I dreamed of my great-grandfather's gold. I want to marry Tsonka, the priest's daughter, but I can't afford to shave, let alone get married. It's only my great-grandfather's treasure that will fix me.' And he spat on his hands again and grabbed the spade. The crowd dispersed.

By evening, the whole house had collapsed, but there was no sign of any treasure. Marin sat on the pile of rubble and looked at the stars in the sky. Until now, he'd been a poor wretch. Now he was a poor wretch and a fool. There wasn't much left for him except to jump in the well, head first. Then someone touched him on the shoulder. It was Tsonka.

'We'll sleep in the hayloft tonight,' she said. 'If tomorrow Dad still doesn't want to wed us, we'll go next door to the village and ask the priest there instead. I heard what you were up to. Why didn't you ask me first, before you pulled your house down? But never mind, if you love me so much, we'll build a new house.'

The next morning, Marin got up first, kissed Tsonka who looked like a nymph in the hay, poured a bucket of water over his head and started piling up the stones again for a new house. Then suddenly he saw the coins. A pot packed full of pure gold coins.

Cardilescu

THIS HAPPENED FIFTEEN YEARS AGO, ON A FINE APRIL DAY.

'There's a great big pain in your heart, boy,' said the Gypsy woman on the park bench as I walked past her. 'Give us a fag and I'll tell you everything.'

She had the face of an old pirate, a silver coin on a string around her neck and a bleeding heart and arrow tattoo on her right wrist.

She stunned me with that comment. The day before, I had broken up with Ely – for ever! And now I was dragging myself around the ashen streets like a battered dog, chain-smoking and looking for a gun to shoot myself with. What else was I going to do without my little, speckle-eyed Ely? I gave the Gypsy woman a cigarette and sat next to her on the bench.

'Nice hand you got there, boy. But a great big pain in your

heart! Did your girl dump you or something?'

The Gypsy woman glanced at me with her violet eyes and the silver coin on her neck flickered. I swallowed dryly and nodded.

'Now listen to me. There's only one cure to fix a big great pain like that. I got it and it's a plant that goes by the name of *cardilescu*. It was for my son, but I'll give it to you 'cause I see you're in a bad way. Costs money, though.'

'How much?' I asked.

The Gypsy woman extracted a little rag from her bosom, unwrapped it and showed me a tiny dry root, as big as a fingernail.

'For you, special price, twenty lev.'

I had eleven lev only.

'Take it, it's from me,' she said. I gave her the money, took the *cardilescu* and went home.

By the entrance to my tower block there was a florist, and I dropped in to see her to show her the little root.

'Pure geranium,' she said. 'I'm more than sure. I've been dealing with flowers all my life.'

I almost threw the *cardilescu* out, but changed my mind at the last minute and put it back in my pocket. As soon as I got home, the phone rang.

'Still cross?' said Ely. "Cause I'm not. You want to get together?'

I wanted it so much that our getting together continues to this day.

The Executioner

THE GALLOWS STILL STANDS IN THE VILLAGE TO THIS DAY.
In the last forty years, the beams have gone grey like stone and
the square around has turned into a wasteland. Once in a while,
some quick-footed little old woman, all dressed in black like a
mole, will stop and look at it from a distance and cross herself.
In the morning, Vando the goatherd passes through here, and
his goats always stop for a moment, then lift their heads in panic
and rush ahead madly, and the tinkling of their bells fills the
marbled winter silence shot through with the frozen threads of
chimney smoke.

Forty years ago, they hanged Pavel here. Nobody knew who
kicked the barrel and so nobody got convicted. How do you
convict an entire village? And anyway, Pavel had committed a
great sin. He came here as an outsider one day, to do odd jobs.

He'd go and dig all day, then he'd get wasted in the evening and so he never got to keep a job. He lived like a homeless dog in a derelict house with no water or electricity. Otherwise he was a handsome fellow, blond and tough, and when he was sober, he worked enough for four men. One day, the soap-maker's widow took him under her wing. Pavel still drank, but he stopped wallowing in the ditch, as it were, and now his shirt collars were washed. And just when people thought that something good might come of him, the village awoke to the news that the soap-maker's widow was dead – strangled in her own house. The whole village passed through the church to bid her farewell, and the whole village went to the graveyard, because the widow had been a good and compassionate woman, even if she had a mind of her own. Pavel was drunk as usual, and didn't remember a thing, no matter how much they interrogated him. So the men tied him up, knocked together a gallows, and at sunset on the day of the widow's funeral they hanged him. And they buried him next to the widow. When the people's militia came, they talked to everyone, but they never found out who had strangled the widow, and who had kicked the barrel under Pavel's feet.

Forty years have passed. The square has turned into a wasteland. Only Vando passes through with his goats, looks around, brings out a canister and takes a long, bitter gulp from it. Then he drives the herd onwards, up the hill to the graveyard. And while the goats pull at twigs along the low graveyard fence, he hops inside, sits between the two graves, and his cracked fingers stroke the porcelain face of the widow with a long braid over her shoulder. Then he pours a few drops of rakia on the earth and takes another drink, and as he drinks, his lumpy throat turns up to the sky and shakes, and it shakes for a long time, long after the rakia is gone, and you would never know whether Vando was laughing or crying.

The Rag-and-Bone Man

ONCE A WEEK, A MIGHTY VOICE SHOOK THE NEIGHBOUR-hood. 'Buying old and used goooods,' the voice called, and the glass in the windows tinkled as if in a storm.

The old lady waited anxiously for this moment. She'd show up at the window and wave her arms, then go down into the street.

The rag-and-bone man was well over sixty, with a brick-red neck, and carried two enormous leather saddlebags. He'd drop the saddlebags on the pavement and embark on a long, elaborate haggle with the lady. He examined her deceased husband's mothball-sprinkled anorak and jacket, the stone-hard shoes, the officer's coat, the faded bowler hat, the glassless pocket watch, the brown-spotted twelve-piece cutlery set, the heavy little rakia glasses, the ancient razor with a cracked bone handle. Then he produced a wad of small, battered banknotes and some of the objects went into his bottomless saddlebags. But still the lady wouldn't leave him alone.

'You could've shaved, you know,' she'd say to him. 'You could've sewn your shirt button on. Instead of going around like some rag-and-bone salesman!' And she'd burst into a laughter fragrant like dry carnations.

But the salesman didn't lose his cool.

'I buy up old women too, you know. Jump in the saddlebags if you're keen.'

The woman stepped away from the fearful, oxen-like saddlebags, but still didn't leave.

'What's your name, what shall I call you?'

'Call me Raggy, short for rag-and-bone man.'

The lady tugged shyly at her paisley collar.

'And where do you live, Raggy?'

He was lifting the saddlebags onto his shoulders again.

'At the end of the world. In a shack.'

'And do you have a little garden?'

'I have a little garden, and a little water fountain too.'

The lady smoothed her white hair and blushed.

'And, er… do you live alone?'

'Yep, alone with my fate.'

She looked around, asked Raggy to wait a minute and rushed up the stairs again. After a little while, she came back carrying a bundle. She had put on a flower-printed dress and a white headscarf.

'Well, you said you buy up old women too,' she said quietly. And off they went, side by side.

The Signalman

GENE LIVES IN A TALL TOWER BLOCK IN THE RESIDENTIAL complex of Youth 1. The block looks like something out of a cult novel – one entrance only, broken elevators and walls scratched with smutty graffiti.

Gene is a signalman. He works shifts at a small railway station where no trains stop. Otherwise, he writes. Years ago, he published a slim book, and the critics patted him on the shoulder and even gave him a literary debut prize. The prize is a tiny bronze Pegasus. Gene polishes it every day and it shines like gold.

Gene is a single parent of two kiddies. The elder daughter is a top student, but the son is a bit of a pain.

Sometimes, I drop in to see Gene.

'Are you writing?' I ask.

'No,' he says and swallows, and his neck tendons stick out painfully. 'My heating bill alone is five hundred levs. They cut off my phone. How can I write in these conditions? I've sold my entire library. I sold the Pegasus too. And the Chekhov.'

'You shouldn't have sold the Chekhov,' I say.

Gene lives on the twelfth floor, and from his window I can see the road to the airport.

'I've got to go,' he says. 'I'm on night shift. Got a cigarette?'

I give him the whole packet and leave. It's dusk, it's snowing and the winter seems endless. Cars crawl along the streets. Tsarigradsko Boulevard is a bad joke – nothing but potholes, dirty slush and darkness. I get off at the Pliska bus stop to take the bus home. But beforehand, I decide to have a look at the book stalls. I haven't bought books for ages, I just look at them now.

At one stall, I spot the blue fabric-bound backs of Chekhov's six collected volumes, and I wipe the snow from them.

'Can I help you?' asks the seller, and wipes her nose with her sleeve. She is all wrapped up in scarves.

'I'll take them,' I say. 'How much?'

Mississippi

BIMBO HAD BEEN A TAXI DRIVER FOR EIGHT YEARS. HE worked at night, because it paid better. In his eight years as a taxi driver, he'd managed to quit smoking and lose his hair, but he hadn't managed to buy a new car. His Trabant still huffed and puffed in the dark streets of Sofia, and Bimbo boasted to his clients about the indestructible nature of Trabant hinge bolts, the toughest thing in the world. His night-time clients came in all hues – there were skylarks among them, there were political commentators, fire-eaters and tombstone-makers. There was plenty of work, but there was also plenty of waiting at the taxi stands. While he waited for customers, Bimbo froze in the car, snoozed, listened to the radio and felt like the night would never end. It was as if the night was longer than the Mississippi river. Bimbo knew from crosswords that the

Mississippi is America's longest river.

Thank God for Tanya. Tanya was the radio host of a night programme. Her voice floated under Bimbo's closed eyelids like a gull under a leaden sky.

'I'm Tanya, and I'll be with you for the next three hours. When I was a child, I was often alone because Mum and Dad worked night shifts. I talked to myself so I wouldn't go bananas. I invented a friend and I talked to him all night. I'm Tanya, and you are the friends I'm inventing tonight.'

Bimbo stroked his green car radio. He so wanted to see this Tanya in person. And suddenly, he decided he would. Why not buy three red roses, park outside the radio station, wait for Tanya to come out, give her the roses and offer her a free lift home? That's right, that's exactly what he was going to do. He looked at his watch, rushed to get the roses, started the engine and struggled up the hill to the radio station. He joined the line of green-eyed taxis along the pavement and fixed his eyes on the door of the building.

The radio song ended and Tanya said: 'Now I'll say goodbye until midnight tomorrow. I'll be on time. You be on time too. I'll leave you with a little poem: "We made a raft from logs / We hardly made it through the night." Ta-ta.'

The taxi drivers started coming out of their cars and lighting up cigarettes. After five minutes, a girl came out of the building. The drivers rushed towards her.

'It's my turn tonight, Tanya,' they shouted over each other. 'My turn, over here!'

Tanya jumped into a taxi, the lucky driver hooted his horn proudly and the other drivers went back to their cars. And off they went, in a nightly procession. Right at the back, huffing and puffing and howling for dear life in third gear, was a little Trabant.

Casablanca

THEIR LITTLE HOUSE WAS THE LAST REMAINING HOUSE IN
the suburb. In just a couple of years, dozens of tower blocks had
shot up all over the place. At night, they glittered like transat-
lantic cruise ships. Mr and Mrs Sarafov's little one-storey house
stood out and spoiled the view.

Mr and Mrs Sarafov were very old. In the evening, they came
out for a walk and shuffled with mouselike steps among the cars
parked on the pavement. They were stiff, like cut-outs from
some cracked old sepia photograph. Entrepreneurs couldn't wait
for them to die – it was a known fact that the old couple had no
heirs. Then, in the spot where the little house stood, a whole
new high-rise could be built. But Mr and Mrs Sarafov wouldn't
die. Day after day they would come out on their walk, their
hands entwined and transparent like the wings of sea-horses.

She carried a dainty umbrella against the sun, and he wore pointy black shoes, shiny like the surface of a grand piano.

They said the two of them had met a thousand years ago in their high-school days, at a screening of *Casablanca*. Since then, they'd seen the film hundreds of times. Young couples in the neighbourhood used this name as a code whenever they wanted a bit of privacy – and they would never be turned away from the little house.

One morning, Mr and Mrs Sarafov were found dead in their house. Their tiny bodies had been bound in transparent tape from top to bottom. They looked like sea-horses who'd fallen asleep in dewy grass. The beat-up municipal funeral van took them away without much ado. The next day, a bulldozer demolished their house.

Now in its place there is a gigantic nightclub. Impressive, blood-red neon letters spell out its name on the façade: CASABLANCA. The letters pulse in the night like hearts. Every night, limousines spill out laughing couples who disappear inside the silver gate as if boarding a spaceship. The women carry dainty little umbrellas and the men wear pointy black shoes, shiny like the surface of a grand piano. They say the most expensive piece of entertainment here is the private screening of *Casablanca*.

Apparently, they screen it round the clock in an exclusive private theatre, for the enjoyment of very select clients only.

Paris

EVERYTHING SEEMED EASY BACK THEN BECAUSE I WAS twenty-three. In the daytime I was a university student, and at night I was a psychiatric orderly. I wrapped up my night duties in an hour or two. I distributed the food, then collected the dirty dishes, washed up, waited for the patients to finish watching their TV drama, and when they'd gone to bed I washed the corridor, took out the rubbish bags and came back up the stairs, whistling past the stone heads of the fathers of psychiatry. In the office, I took out my notebook and cigarettes and knocked off a story in a couple of hours. The endings were the easiest part for me. They'd hit the reader on the head like a hammer. Then, like any writer, I needed to share with someone the miracle of creation. So I'd call the duty nurse and we'd talk into the morning. The psychiatric nurses were social creatures. They also wore their white uniforms with nothing underneath.

That night, the nurse on duty was Valeria. She was ten years older than me and her skin was smooth like carbon paper. I knew two things about her: she was divorced, and she'd once been a rhythmic gymnast. She sat on the high hospital bed and leaned her back against the wall, taking care to cover with the white uniform her gymnast thighs. Like all nurses, she abused make-up but the soot-black, shiny eyes suited her.

'So,' Valeria said. 'Are you going to write a story for me?'

I poured an inch of medicinal alcohol into two small tin jugs, lit them for a few seconds, squeezed some lemon in and handed her a drink. I swallowed mine in one go.

'I am,' I said. 'Just say what you'd like. You have the unique opportunity to order your own story. With a stunning ending.'

Valeria took a slow sip from her jug and kept turning the cheap plastic bracelet around her right wrist.

'I want to be in Paris!' she said suddenly. 'I want to sit at a table outside a bistro with large windows. The pavement is just washed, the river Seine is reflected in the window and I have a big straw hat. A man in a light-coloured suit and smelling of pipe tobacco approaches from behind and offers me a bunch of gerberas. I love gerberas.'

I poured myself some more alcohol from the dark green, two-litre bottle and drank it quickly.

'Done,' I said. 'No problem. Paris is just my thing. But I have to see your legs first, so I can write about them well. A story without beautiful legs is not a story. Even a good ending can't save it.'

The spirit had gone to my head fast, but Valeria was humouring me and laughing at my rantings. At that point, someone bellowed. That was Spass, who lived behind a grille door in a small room at the end of the corridor. We fed him through the grille. He'd take the tin jug, sit on the floor and feed his face. Then he'd throw the cleaned-out jug onto the mosaic floor.

Valeria became serious.

'You've got the key, haven't you? Let him walk in the corridor a bit,' she pleaded.

'He's OK where he is.'

'The doctor is upstairs. Nobody will know. Just for a bit. You know, sometimes he has such a sad look.'

'Spass is an animal,' I said. 'Let's talk about something else.'

And I started reading her my latest story. At three in the morning, time stops. Valeria's eyes are full of long, broken rays. I can hear the nightingales in the garden outside. Spass has also gone quiet. It's so quiet, I can hear Valeria's breathing. I finished reading.

'I'm going to sleep,' Valeria said and got up. I stood in her way and embraced her awkwardly. She didn't budge. She wasn't helping me, but she wasn't impeding me either. This emboldened me.

'Wait,' she said, and moved aside to undo the buttons of her uniform. I grabbed the keys with shaking hands and locked the office door. Then I turned the lights off.

I was woken by shouts in the canteen. Something was happening. Valeria wasn't there. I jumped up from the bed, splashed water on my eyes and pushed the door handle. It was unlocked. My keys weren't there. A few patients were trying to restrain Spass. His hand gripped a stool leg. There was dried foam on his mouth.

'He hit Valeria on the head,' said Vladko, one of the other patients holding Spass down. 'He hit her many times.'

I ran down the corridor. Valeria was lying on the mosaic floor outside the bathroom. A few doctors from the morning shift were fussing around her. I couldn't see her for the crowd pressing around her. All I glimpsed was her hair, clumped with blood. Then they lifted her onto a stretcher and took her away.

I never saw Valeria again. After a while, I heard that she had been in hospital for a long time, then she'd gone into a sanatorium, and finally she took early retirement. Spass also disappeared after the incident. He was moved to a remote asylum.

Valeria, I have finally fulfilled my promise, I have written a story for you. Except that I don't know how to end it. So I'll leave it like this. All I know is that it will be called 'Paris'.

Storks

OLD TYRES WERE BURNING AT THE END OF THE VILLAGE again, and the sunset was barely visible behind the thick black smoke. It was a nice day today, old Patso thought to himself, it was warm for the first time in ages. There had been no snow for a week now, but it was still cold, cold to the bone. But today, the weather was softening up, and in the places where grass was going to grow, the soil began to squelch. All day, old Patso pottered about in the courtyard. He didn't do all that much, but he did manage to collect all the debris and the firewood, rearrange the roof tiles bent by the cold, make a gutter for the coming rains so they wouldn't flood the path – and that was it for today. Mostly, he was enjoying the sun and feeling his back warm up under his cardigan. Even Caesar the dog stirred, and walked on stumbling legs from one end of the fence to the other, his chain rattling like a convict's shackles. Caesar had barely made it through the winter. He was just skin and bones. Lyubo will be angry with me if he sees him like this, Patso thought guiltily. Lyubo had brought Patso to the village three years ago. But this winter was very tough, and the mush of bread crusts and water Patso made for the dog in a military can would freeze over on the way between the house and the shed.

Old Patso looked at the tall elm in the churchyard next door. For ten years now there had been a stork's nest up there, and hearing the clatter of beaks each time was a great joy for old Patso because he knew that a male and a female had come to roost. Everybody has secrets, and old Patso's secret was the belief that once the storks were here, he'd make it to the end of the year. That's why, when the weather got milder around Lent, he would lift his eyes up to the elm to look out for the storks. They had come earlier in previous years, he thought, and he spat out bitter saliva.

Their house was well situated, next to the church. They had a nice yard and until a year or two ago, while his wife was still holding up, they'd kept a vine there, as well as an allotment outside the village. But allotments were often burgled these days. Besides, his wife had collapsed after her stroke, and now went around the kitchen gingerly or sat outside on the bench by the window. Sometimes she got on his nerves so much with her pursed, beak-like mouth that he felt like smacking her with the back of his hand and growling at her: Pull yourself together, woman!

Now her birdlike twitter startled him out of his reverie. Stoina was standing at the doorstep and saying something to him with one half of her face, while the other half was frozen and foreign like the face of a pharaoh. He got closer to her and picked out among the twitter the word 'Lyubo', and here he lost his temper.

'What are you on about?' he yelled, but when he saw that she was about to cry, he felt bad. And to hide his upset, he started wiping his own watering, ageing eyes with the sleeve of his cardigan. Then he heard the car engine out in the street. Someone turned it off, slammed the car door and tried to open the little wooden gate of the house yard. Old Patso went to see who it was, and ran into Lyubo.

'Goodness me!' he said. He was overwhelmed with joy and went to look for Stoina, to share the joy with her, but realised he hadn't actually greeted his son, so he turned to him and took him in like only a father can do with a son – from top to bottom, all at once.

'Goodness you,' Lyubo boomed. 'Why don't you come out to greet your guests? I was knocking for ages, and nobody came.'

He quickly hugged his father and leaned against the painted wall.

'Why didn't you ring us, son? That way we'd know to welcome you properly.'

'Why, why? 'Cause I'm just dropping in. I've only got half an hour.'

'Half an hour! You're not going to stay overnight?'

'I'm in a hurry. It's work. How's Mum?'

'Hang on, I'll tell her you're here, she'll be glad.'

And he shouted: 'Stoina, our Lyuben's here, come and see who's here!'

'Don't shout. Don't tell her I'm here, she'll cry.'

'What do you mean, don't tell her? She has to know. You must have some soup, we've got some nettle soup…'

'I told you, I'm here for work. But I'm running behind, it's late and I don't know how I'm going to finish it all…'

'Come and sit down. We'll think of something.'

They went to the door of the house. When she saw him, his mother broke down in tears and embraced his elbow. Tears poured from her left eye, while her right eye stared austerely into the distance, towards the church bell tower.

Old Patso brought out a little table and two chairs and the two men sat down on them while Stoina took her place on the bench under the window. Lyubo took out his cigarettes and gave one to his father. Old Patso took it, tapped its end on his wrecked thumbnail like an old smoker, then wetted it with his tongue, tore off the filter and inhaled hard.

'Now listen.' Lyubo raised his head to the darkening sky. 'You can do this job for me. I've brought everything, it's all ready to go. You have to stick some posters around the village. At the village hall, at the school, at the church, at the bus stop, at the barber's. Is the barber still there?'

'No.'

'OK then, down the pub. On the telegraph poles. Where else?'

'Can't put them up at the bus stop, that's where they glue the death notices. They're one on top of the other, thick like pastry, you can't put anything on top.'

'OK. Wherever you can.'

'What are these posters, anyway?'

'Posters like any others. You know, with elections coming up and everything. So I signed up for it. They pay. Why wouldn't I do it?'

'Well, we'll do it if we have to.'

Lyubo looked at his mother and she broke down again. He stroked her shoulder and got up.

'I'll be going then. Wait, I'll bring the posters.'

He went to the car and came back with a canvas bag full of rolled-up posters, a plastic bucket full of glue and a roller-brush, all brand new and shiny.

'The glue's ready, you don't need to add water or anything. Just spread it on and stick it up. Spread it on and stick it up. At the more obvious places, 'cause apparently they're going round to check it's been done properly, the motherfuckers.'

'Fine. I'll do it.'

'I'll be off, then.'

Lyubo kissed his mother and was gone round the corner of the house. Old Patso rushed after him. They went out into the street next to the car.

'Well, Lyubo, son. Try and drop in more often. We haven't seen you for a year, since your mother's stroke. You didn't see Caesar, either. He was waiting for you. He only just made it through the winter.'

'I'll see him next time. All right then…'

'Safe journey.'

When the noise of the engine had died away, old Patso lifted his face and listened. He stayed like that for a long time. Then he let the door latch down and went in.

Over the Mountains

CHRISTOPHER LINER ARRIVED IN SOFIA JUST AFTER THE New Year celebrations. His mission was to find the kidnapped swine girl and buy the story rights for a book and a film. He had a decent budget for it, but even so, his production company in London had warned him that these things are still very chaotic and unpredictable in Bulgaria.

It was dark when the British Airways flight landed, so he took a taxi to his downtown hotel where he had a room booked. The taxi driver had three-day stubble so thick he looked as if he'd smeared his face with tar, and he wore a leather sombrero.

'Do you speak English?' Liner asked in English.

'Just say what you've got to say,' the driver grinned and turned round abruptly, the razor-sharp edge of his hat catching Liner in the eyebrow. He spoke in Bulgarian. 'You all come here and you get verbal diarrhoea. Motherfuckers.' Then he added in English, 'Yes, speak English! Yes, speak English.'

'What's your name?'

'Listen here, buddy,' the driver said in Bulgarian. 'I don't speak bloody English 'cause I'm at the wheel from dawn till dusk, from dusk till dawn. I don't have time to take a piss, you stupid bastard. Mum and Dad were poor proletarians so I didn't go to the English college, your motherfucker.'

'Kak tebya zovut?' Liner recalled a phrase from his English–Russian phrasebook. He got it at the last moment in London and read through it on the flight, although they'd warned him that despite the similarities, the two Slavic languages were completely different.

'Menya zovut svinskii but,' the driver laughed – using an old Bulgarian–Russian joke – and the sharp edge of his hat ripped at Liner's eyebrow again, in the same spot. 'And kak tebya zovut?'

'Christopher Liner,' the Englishman smiled through his eyebrow pain. And at this point, the driver did something strange. He let go of the wheel, locked his hands behind his head and burst out into a laughter so monstrous he looked like a hippo who was having his nails clipped. It was a miracle the car kept going in a straight line. 'I knew it,' he said when he had calmed down and grabbed the wheel again. 'I knew your name was Shitface, what else would an arsehole like you be called? How do you do, Mister Liner?'

Christopher Liner paid 40 euros for the ride, which was four times the going rate, but he didn't know it. He checked into his room, looked at his brow, changed his clothes and went to the bar downstairs. In the bar, it smelled of expensive pipe tobacco. After a couple of drinks, his eyebrow stopped hurting and he turned to look at the two dancing girls. The blonde one was gorgeous, but too luscious for his refined tastes. Her thighs were bulky like a weightlifter's, and Liner was so chilled at the thought of how easily those thighs could strangle a weedy, tipsy, red-headed Englishman that he stopped looking at her. The dark-haired girl was another matter altogether. Her slim body was so flexible that Liner felt his crotch tense up. He ordered a third drink and asked the waiter to call the girl to his table, if it was convenient. The waiter explained that it was only convenient in fifteen minutes, when the programme finished. Liner nodded and, contrary to his habits, took a huge gulp from his drink.

In fifteen minutes, he could hardly wait. He'd had two more drinks. Finally the girl got down from the pole and disappeared. He shut his eyes and leaned his head back. He felt like a man for the first time in ages.

For years now Liner's sex life had been a desert. He was married with two grown-up children. He hadn't felt anything for his wife for a long time. She was an ecological activist and lived a separate life. Contrary to the Bulgarian preconceptions about Englishmen, he hadn't turned gay, but his sex drive had been reduced to nothing, as if he'd been switched off. In the last year he'd had half a dozen encounters with prostitutes, but they had taken place after large amounts of alcohol and therefore he remembered almost nothing. True, sometimes he saw women in the street whose beauty took his breath away, but those were occasional embers in the ashes of his sexuality.

He felt the girl's presence from her body's heat, and he opened his eyes. He knew that the first eye-contact would be decisive. The girl's face was narrow and intelligent. Her black hair was cropped very short. She had put on a shiny, cobweb-thin top and a short skirt. When she sat down and crossed her legs, her thighs were so beautifully flattened that Liner's heart began to ache.

'Do you speak English?' he asked, fearful that she might not – he had so much to say. He felt his breath heating up, his blood running slowly in his manly arteries and he wanted to talk about politics, sex and the lack of sex, even about poetry, although he hadn't read any in a long time, and about loving her and protecting her.

'Yes, I do,' the girl said and continued in Bulgarian. 'I under-stand everything, but how about I speak in Bulgarian and you in English, and we'll still understand each other. I know what you all want. You pretend you want to fuck, but what you really want is tenderness.'

She stroked his neck with a long manicured fingernail.

'Do you understand?'

'Can I take you for the whole night?'

'Yes,' the girl said. 'But it will be much more expensive.'

'It doesn't matter.'

In the morning, Christopher Liner woke up alone and buck naked. He went to the door, which was unlocked. He locked it and crossed over to the window. There was a brown street below, clogged with cars and people in dark coats. He checked his wallet and his passport – everything was in its place. Then suddenly he was flooded by the memory of the incredible sex he'd had with the girl. He hadn't had sex like that even in his student years. There'd been only one such experience before – during a holiday in Kenya, with the daughter of the maid at the plantation where they'd stayed, and he'd kept the memory of that girl, violet-black and smooth like the inside of a shell, with antelope-like eyes. And he remembered last night clearly, which was remarkable in itself. His hangover was light and euphoric. But what was her name? She'd told him, and he couldn't remember it now. He knew that prostitutes don't usually give their real names, but instead use a few international ones, and yet hers was a local Bulgarian name. While he showered, he was struck with horror at the thought of never seeing that girl again, just because he'd forgotten her name. He dressed quickly and went downstairs where he had orange juice, coffee, bacon and eggs. When his sense of dignity as a royal subject was restored, he asked the waiter if he could talk to the manager of the bar. The waiter nodded and soon, a man appeared, with a parting in his hair and eyelids heavy like a crocodile's.

'I was with one of your girls last night,' Christopher Liner said slowly. 'I'd like to see her again.'

'No problem,' the manager said. 'I'll send her to your room.'

Liner just about ran up the stairs. He unlocked his room, took a look at himself in the mirror, made his bed and sprayed himself with deodorant for the second time. A few moments later, someone knocked at the door. A small, swarthy creature with short, woolly hair stepped in. She looked at him and said 'Hello' in English. Liner froze. She wasn't his girl. The voice wasn't the same and she generally wasn't the same.

'I've forgotten your name. What's your name?' he asked.

'My name is Stacey,' the girl said slowly, as if reading from a phrasebook.

No, it wasn't the right name. He couldn't remember what it was, but it wasn't this. He'd repeated it all night, that name. And anyway, the voice was different, the girl was different. They were having him on.

'OK,' he said. 'Everything's OK.' He patted the girl on the cheek and gave her a 20-euro note. She seemed surprised, then she lifted her top and showed him her young, goaty breasts.

'OK, OK,' Liner repeated, and pushed her out the door.

'It's not enough,' the girl said. 'Twenty euro more.'

Liner gave her another 20-euro note from his wallet, locked the door after her and lay down on his bed with his shoes on. It was time to give up on feelings and concentrate on his mission – to track down the captive swine girl.

The story had appeared online in the Bulgarian media and had reached Liner's production agency in London. It went like this: a beautiful young woman, just out of high school, disappears mysteriously from her small mountain town in the Rodopi ranges. Nobody claims her because her mother works as an old people's carer in Greece, and her father is a desperate alcoholic. Meanwhile, in a separate investigation, two journalists from a provincial newspaper discover a network of illegal meat-processing joints, and eventually come across a pig farm in the mountains, owned by a local. Imagine their surprise when they discover that one single girl looks after the dozens of swine, living among them in the stinking mud. Their surprise turned to astonishment when it became clear that this was the vanished girl. On top of that, she was not only a slave labourer, she was also the owner's sex slave. He'd come up the mountain regularly, to keep an eye on his swine, bring provisions and sate his sexual appetite. The journalists had depicted the shocking scenes of repeated rape, with the bristly pigs and the jagged mountain cliffs as sole witnesses to these crimes. The article ended on a positive note: the owner was being prosecuted, and the girl had returned to her native town.

Christopher Liner had the contact details for the provincial newspaper and the two journalists who'd written the article a year ago. He phoned the British Embassy, hired a car with a driver and a translator and confirmed his prearranged afternoon appointment with the two journalists.

During the journey, he looked out at the countryside with interest. Fortunately, he had respectful companions who didn't bother him with unnecessary talk. The driver was an aged man with a shaved neck and extremely hairy nostrils. He was clearly desperate to keep his well-paid job. The translator was young, probably a recent graduate, and had a picturesque carbuncle under his mouth and slightly out-of-focus eyes. He was trying to be confident to compensate for his inexperience, but unfortunately this only made his stammer more obvious. His name was Bobby, and the driver was called Stoyan.

They stopped at a Shell petrol station to refuel and fortify themselves in the café. Liner asked them to get him a coffee with milk, and headed for the toilets. They were out of order. A cleaner woman with metal teeth and bare blue heels directed him to the building complex next door. It was huge – with a restaurant and a hotel – and it was closed. Outside there was a broken children's playground, tables covered with plastic sheets and rusted, empty stalls. The toilet was at the bottom of a wide, operatic staircase. At the entrance, Liner had to jump over a huge brown puddle with bits of ice and cigarette packets floating in it. Then he found himself in a giant, echoing hall full of dozens of sinks and mirrors. Clearly, this place had been thriving once upon a time, otherwise the toilets wouldn't be larger than those at the Albert Hall. But that must have been a while ago because now the wall tiles were broken off and the rusty, blurry mirrors were like windows to the Underworld. And inside this giant fridge, a child sat at a small table and wrote something in a notebook. Next to the notebook there was a saucer with a few coins, carefully folded napkins and a small, propped-up piece of cardboard that said '20'. The child looked at Liner, startled. Liner searched his pockets and found a one-euro coin which he put in the saucer. The child got up, picked up the coin and dropped it in his pocket. He was a small boy, and the pearl of snot hanging at the tip of his nose wouldn't fall.

'What's your name?' Christopher Liner asked on his way out. The child remained standing. Then suddenly he tore off a page from his notebook and handed it to Liner, who automatically folded it and put it in his pocket without looking at it. The little boy stared at him without blinking. He was dressed in a long man's jacket that reached down to his knees.

Back in the café, Stoyan and Bobby were visibly anxious. There were all sorts in the café – respectable, well-dressed people along with tramp-like types wrapped up in colourful shawls with beer bottles sticking out of their pockets and the whiff of urine around them. Most of the patrons looked at Liner with undisguised curiosity and he couldn't help but feel as if he'd done something wrong. He quickly drank his milky coffee and off they went again.

They arrived in the regional town of Haskovo just in time for their meeting with the journalists. They parked in a square hemmed in by corrugated iron. A man with wild eyes and a green fluorescent jacket moved among the parked cars, and immediately set upon them with a stub of invoices, tearing off page after page like a magician until Stoyan managed to calm him down. He stayed in the car while Liner and Bobby headed off to the Artists' and Writers' Club in town. After a few minutes, they found themselves in a low-ceilinged, smoky room with low, plush banquettes covered with cigarette burns and a billiard table covered with empty beer crates. They'd just sat at one of the low coffee tables when two men appeared from the other end of the establishment. The gutted seats were so desperately uncomfortable that Liner made three attempts to get up before he managed it, helping himself with his hands and twisting himself around. As he rose, he found himself in the arms of one of the two guys. He was short but had an iron handshake.

'Shilenderov,' he introduced himself. He wore an overcoat that reached down to his ankles.

'Ulev,' offered the other journalist. He was tall and broad like Muhammad Ali at the height of his career, and although his colleague's overcoat would have fitted him perfectly, he preferred to wear a short, worn-out leather jacket which made him look like a pathetic clown.

Then they all sat down around the table. While Liner was trying to memorise all the names, Shilenderov blew away the thick layer of cigarette ash from the table and called the waitress. Four vodkas instantly landed before them.

'Cheers then,' Shilenderov said. 'Welcome. Here's to doing business together.'

Bobby tasted his vodka and started translating. After a few more sips, his English became smooth like that of a BBC presenter. Soon, the story took shape. The girl, Ruzha, is responsible for several dozen pigs. Her day begins before dawn. She has to boil water in the two big cauldrons, cut some nettles with a cleaver, salt and stir the mixture, then carry the feed to the sty in two big buckets. It takes many trips, and she goes backwards and forwards. Entering the sty is dangerous in itself, as the savage, hungry pigs could easily push her down and stampede over her. When she pours the feed in the buckets, the pigs start eating and calm down, and at that point Ruzha can move on to the cleaning. With a spade as heavy as a stone, she has to gather all the dung in a pile, then flip it over the fence. By dawn she's already exhausted, but she can't afford even a moment's rest. Before she knows it, it'll be four in the afternoon, and Djendo Vezenkov will be here in his jeep. She has to wait for him at the top of the hill, washed and neat. He drives the jeep into the narrow courtyard, and she walks behind it in the hard furrows of earth. He gets out, pats her cheek proprietarily and unloads the bags of ground corn. Then he beckons to her and together they head off to the pigsty. Djendo has to check up on his pigs. When he's reassured that all is well, he turns to Ruzha and, without warning, he pushes his thumb, big like a gun barrel, inside her mouth. Ruzha has to suck on his thumb and not only that, but she has to show sublime pleasure. If she doesn't, too bad for her. Once, he became enraged at the lack of sublime pleasure on her face, stripped her naked, pushed her onto her knees and raped her right there, in full sight of the pigs, on the piss-and-shit-smeared floor of the sty.

Shilenderov made a sign at the waitress and four more vodkas landed on their table.

'It's a saga,' he said. 'A real Balkan saga. With the Rodopi ranges as a backdrop. Emir Kusturica, move over.'

'Aha,' Ulev agreed. 'That's right.'

Christopher Liner was tense as a spring. He was trying hard to keep his clarity of thought despite the vodka. Bobby was very flushed.

'So where are Ruzha and Djendo now?' he asked. Shilenderov and Ulev looked at each other.

'Ruzha is back in her home town, with her grandmother,' Shilenderov said. 'And Djendo is being prosecuted.'

'What, they haven't convicted him yet, after a whole year?' Liner said, amazed.

'Here in Bulgaria things move slowly.' Shilenderov smiled. 'But now, with help from our powerful brothers in England, we can speed them up.'

'Aha,' Ulev said. The vodka was having an extraordinary effect on him. After one glass, his vague expression had been replaced by a dark brooding force. He was also very heavy, and his hundred and twenty kilos had sunk into Liner's couch, so that Liner kept sliding towards him.

'And why didn't Ruzha run away?' Liner asked.

'Well, you must have read some psychology books,' Shilenderov said politely. 'You know about the so-called Stockholm syndrome, where the victim is so paralysed by her captor that, paradoxically, she becomes dependent on him. Even the smallest signs of attention from him mean the world to her, including sexual violence. Factor in the victim's extreme youth and inexperience, and there you have it...'

With a magician's sleight of hand, Shilenderov extracted a small folder from his overcoat, placed it on his knee and stroked it.

'It's all here,' he said. 'The whole story. The whole sad story of a Bulgarian girl on the threshold of maturity who leaves school and instead of a ball, gets squealing pigs and hard spade handles. All translated into English.'

'I see,' Liner kept nodding. He couldn't wait to go outside for some fresh air. Shilenderov was staring at him and his eyebrow cut suddenly started hurting again. Shilenderov's stare was as sharp as a poke with a billiard cue.

'Do you have permission to sign the contract?' Shilenderov asked.

Liner pushed himself off the rock-hard thigh of Ulev, who rose above him by half a metre, even though he was seated next to him.

'Not exactly,' he said. 'In fact, it's my task to go location-scouting and draw up a report. I have to get enough information to present to my bosses. I also need your text, of course: it will go into the script. All this will take a few days. I could call you, say, on Friday, and then we can talk about the specifics.'

Shilenderov downed his vodka in one swift gulp, then took a sheet out of the folder and handed it to Liner.

'This is the synopsis. We'll wait for your call.'

He and Ulev rose together. Liner and Bobby followed suit. The journalists nodded, businesslike, shook hands with the Englishman and headed for the exit. The waitress came over to the table.

'She'd like to settle the bill,' Bobby explained.

'Sure,' Liner said, brought out a 20-euro note and stepped outside with a feeling of relief.

Stoyan was sleeping, locked inside the car, but like the

old hand he was, he woke himself up with a single shake of the head. Liner and Bobby got in. Stoyan looked at Liner quizzically.

'Bobby, what's the time?' Liner asked. His internal clock told him it was around ten past four. This was one of his obsessions. He never wore a watch, and he prided himself on knowing exactly what time it was.

'Ten past four,' Bobby said. Liner felt an inrush of confidence. He was beginning to appreciate this balding youth who'd coped so well with his job so far.

'What did you make of those two?' he asked.

Bobby swallowed. He sensed he'd been somehow promoted.

'They're professionals. But quite predatory.'

'What do you suggest we do?'

'I think we should definitely find Ruzha and that guy Djendo.'

'How many kilometres away from her town are we now?'

Stoyan was already looking at a map.

'A hundred and fifty,' he said, and Bobby translated.

'And the swine farm?'

'It's closer, about sixty or seventy kilometres.'

'Right,' Liner said. He was observing an old Gypsy man who kept criss-crossing the square, looking for discarded fags. His aim was to find a new fag before the one in his mouth went out completely, so that he could light one with the other. He was managing very well. 'OK. This is what we're going to do. We go to the town. We find Ruzha. We stay overnight. Tomorrow, on our way back, we'll go via the swine farm.'

Liner sat in the car with his eyes half closed. When the car started swerving, he knew they'd entered the mountainous region. He looked out of the window. It was close to dusk. Snow appeared by the sides of the road. From time to time, they overtook horse carts piled up with wood. After a bend, they hit a long straight bit of road. Liner noticed a female figure on the right-hand side.

'Stop,' he said to Stoyan abruptly. Stoyan went past the woman and pulled over.

'What is she doing on the road?' Liner asked.

'She's selling something,' Bobby said. 'Probably dried black-berries or blueberries. It's one of the things people sell around here.'

Liner got out of the car and Bobby followed close behind him. The woman was a young girl, almost a child. She'd wrapped her head in a woollen headscarf and they couldn't see her hair, but her eyes were so big and shiny that Liner didn't even look at the fruit before he asked Bobby to buy the whole plastic bucket. The girl looked genuinely happy.

'Ask her what her name is,' he said to Bobby.

'Aya,' the girl answered.

'Ask her what she does.'

'She's finished school. Now she looks after six goats. In the summer, she picks wild berries. She wants to study textiles in Plovdiv.'

The girl listened to Bobby's translation with her head slightly cast down. There was no trace of embarrassment in her eyes.

'Would she be insulted if I offered her money? Just like that, for something to buy for herself.'

Bobby looked at the girl carefully and didn't ask her.

'I think she would be,' he said to Liner.

'Ciao,' Liner said to the girl, and saw that her face was covered in freckles. In the muted light of dusk, they looked as if they were made of silver.

'Ciao,' Aya said.

In a few seconds, the little figure disappeared behind the bend.

Christopher Liner stretched his legs out and leaned back, and suddenly realised that his hands were gripping the plastic bucket of dried fruit. It was too dark to see the fruit clearly. It was small, shrivelled and black. He picked up a few and tasted them. They gave him a jolt. They were cold and slightly tart, and they told him about Aya's summer, her running after the goats, her legs scratched by brambles, her shouts and laughter and the end of her childhood.

Soon, they reached the little town. The road turned into a long high street lined with houses. They reached a dimly lit square. On one side of the square there was a dark building with a huge tree in its courtyard. It was probably a church, judging from the cross on the roof, which stood out clearly against the pure green sky. On the other side there was a low building with steamed-up windows. A man came out of the door, went around the corner and they heard the whip-like noise of a strong jet. Then the man blew his nose loudly and went back inside the pub.

'I'll go in and ask about Ruzha,' Bobby offered. Liner nodded. He'd wound down the car window and was enjoying the incredibly pure mountain air. Somewhere in the distance, bells tinkled. Bobby came back with a man.

'This is a neighbour of her grandmother's,' he explained. 'He said he'll take us there.'

The man sat in the back next to Liner and they took off. He exuded alcohol fumes, garlic and sweat. Soon they turned off the main street and up a steep, uneven dirt road. The houses became smaller, more like village houses.

'It's round here somewhere,' the man said, and started feeling for the door handle. He pressed on something which broke with a crack. Bobby got out, went around the car and opened his door from the outside. The little house where they'd stopped was dark, except for a faint light in one of the windows – a TV perhaps.

'Penna, come, open up,' the man shouted.

A door slammed inside, and a woman came out on the small

veranda, switched a light on and came down the steps. She took care to pull her headscarf over her hair.

'Kiro, is that you?' she asked.

"Course it's me, who else? Come, 'cause these folks are looking for you.'

'Good evening,' Bobby greeted her when she came out. 'Sorry about the late visit. We wanted to talk to you.'

'Come in,' the woman said. 'Come in. Goodnight to you, Kiro, and call in tomorrow about the milk.'

Stoyan stayed in the car. Christopher Liner and Bobby went up the stairs and found themselves in a small room, carefully lined with rugs. On the table was a clean plastic cloth. The woman wiped it with the palm of her hand, placed a bowl of walnuts on it, sat in one of the chairs and looked at her visitors. She was small and dressed in a thick black cardigan over which she wore an apron.

'We're looking for Ruzha. We were told you're her grandmother,' Christopher Liner said, and Bobby translated.

'You're looking for Ruzha but she's not here, she's not here,' the old woman said and started rocking in her chair. 'Not here, not here. God will punish that old goat the teacher, who lied to her and tricked her. He'll take her for a bride, he said, for a bride. What do I do, Grandma, Ruzha asked me back then. I said listen to your heart, sweetheart. If you love him, go with him. And she went, my little Ruzha, never to be seen again. Anyway, there's nothing for her here, no lads, no life, only drunks and goats. She would have passed from one pair of hands to another if she'd stayed. So I say, Go to him, sweetheart, if he's on your heart. I'll be called Vezenkova, Grandma, she goes, Ruzha Vezenkova, nice name. So off she goes, my little Ruzha, off she goes, never to be seen again.'

Christopher Liner listened to Bobby's translation but even without it, the woman's intonation told him a great deal.

'And who are you?' the old woman suddenly said, in a severe voice.

Christopher Liner tries to explain, carefully choosing his words, that he's the representative of a film agency in London, that they're looking for new faces. They were going to make Ruzha an actress, she was going to earn money, big money. He was afraid the woman might ask how they knew about Ruzha, but she didn't ask anything.

She got up, threw a little log on the fire and said: 'You can stay the night. I'll get your beds ready.'

And then they heard her puffing and huffing along the corridor for ages, carrying piles of bedding. Christopher Liner was put in a small, whitewashed room. Dried herbs and quince as big as yellow lanterns were spread out on newspapers on the floor. When he woke up in the morning, it took him a while to work out where he was. He looked with interest at the old-fashioned window frame which stood out like a cross against the pink sky, then he looked outside. They were high up, and down below, the town was spread out. He managed to make out the church with its large tree. He dressed, went out into the creaky hallway, opened the front door and went downstairs to wash in the courtyard sink. He cupped his hands and took a sip of water.

'Come and have breakfast,' the old woman beckoned to him from the top of the stairs. Stoyan and Bobby were waiting for him in the kitchen. They had a cup of scorching milk each, and freshly baked cheese pastries which the woman had risen at dawn to make.

'How much money should I leave her?' Christopher whispered to Bobby.

'It must be in levs, she's never seen euros,' Bobby whispered back.

Christopher set a fifty-lev note aside, the equivalent to twenty-five euros. He went to the old woman, made a stiff bow and handed her the banknote. The woman started shaking uncontrollably. She didn't refuse the money, but she didn't take it either. She just stood there and shook. Christopher Liner put the note on the table and hurried down the chipped steps.

Driving out of the town, they came across a herd of goats. They were taking up the whole lane, so the three of them had to wait. At the front of the herd was a large greyish-white goat, twice the size of the she-goats. As he walked, his back swayed like a gondola. One of his horns was broken and a big bell hung from his neck. On each side of the herd were two lambs with red string around their necks. From time to time, the goat turned around and gave his females a heavy once-over. Right at the back was the goatherd, a massive man with a woven woollen overcoat over his shoulders. He held a wooden pole between his elbows and across his back. Soon, the herd turned up a crooked path and spread up the hill like a slowly opening fan.

'Why do the small goats have red string around their necks?' Christopher Liner asked. Bobby was puzzled. He hadn't noticed.

'What did Mr Liner ask?' Stoyan said.

'Why the lambs have red around their necks.'

'It's a local custom. Against evil spells.'

Bobby translated and Liner nodded to show he'd understood, even though he hadn't.

They drove for almost two hours non-stop. Christopher Liner studied the mountainous landscape. The roads were shabby and there were derelict buildings on both sides. They often passed trucks piled up with logs. Roadside cafés flashed past them, with people sitting at tables or on the ground and selling honey and dried fruits of the forest. At one point, they pulled over onto a car island and Bobby and Stoyan looked at the map and discussed something. Then they drove up a steep road which was tarmacked up to the point where it became a dirt road dug out by streams. Stoyan's neck glistened with sweat.

Finally, they came out on a snowy hilltop and stopped.

'The swine farm must be here somewhere,' Bobby said.

Liner stepped out of the car and went over to the edge of the ravine overgrown with a dense beard of pine trees. He looked around. On a fallen log sat a little old man. He had appeared out of nowhere, like a genie. The old man had propped his chin on his walking stick and was calmly looking at them. Liner called out to Bobby and went over to the old man with an arm outstretched in a greeting, then he bounced back.

'It won't bite you,' the old man said.

Liner clenched his teeth and approached again, avoiding eye-contact with the enormous dog that lay at the old man's feet. Liner had never seen a dog like it – it had long hair and black and white spots, a massive round head and ears that seemed to have been cut. His paws were like a giant's fists. The dog observed Liner with interest and a look that made Liner's skin crawl. Bobby was standing at an odd angle, just behind Liner.

'Hello,' the Englishman said at last. 'I'm Liner, Christopher Liner.' His mouth had gone dry.

'God bless you. I'm Bojo. What brings you here?' the old man said.

'We're looking for a man called Djendo Vezenkov,' Bobby said. 'He rears pigs somewhere around here.'

'Yes, there was such a man a while back. What do you need him for?'

Liner pinched his nose and then breathed out noisily.

'We heard he had problems with the law. We want to meet him, and if it seems right, to help him out.'

'There was such a man, Djendo Vezenkov. He threw himself into making money. He built the farm, brought the pigs. He worked round the clock. He was a teacher of literature in some town below. Divorced. He must have been around fifty. But strong – he could carry two bags of cement on his back. He wanted to start a new life, get it right this time. At one point, a girl turned up. Young, like a dewdrop. I say, Djendo, she's too young for you, and he goes, She loves me, Bojo, she loves me. They both worked like troopers, non-stop. They wanted a good life. I looked at the girl and to tell you the truth, I felt sorry for her. Her hands turned to hooves from all the hard labour, scrubbing all day long. When are you going to live your life, girl, I go. And she says, Life is ahead of me, Bojo, I'm still young. But people got jealous of their success. Some officials came, some journalists wrote in the paper about them and it all went to hell. The girl disappeared, Djendo disappeared. The pigs got stolen. One day, half a year ago, I see a jeep. Police. What's going on? Bad stuff, that's what. Djendo'd come back to the ruins of the pig farm and hanged himself. Some shepherds saw him and called the police. So Djendo is no more. You've come too late.'

Liner crouched, broke off a handful of hardened snow and rubbed his forehead with it.

'Let's go,' he said to Bobby and got up. He nodded stiffly at the old man and they headed back to the car.

They arrived in Sofia at dusk. The car pulled up in front of the downtown hotel. The three of them stood on the pavement.

'Bobby, I'll write you a good reference,' Liner said. 'You were brilliant.'

Bobby flushed with pleasure. In the last two days, a golden downy stubble had grown over his face. Liner asked him to book the quickest flight out of Sofia for him, and then call him to confirm. Bobby nodded like a squaddie who'd just been promoted to sergeant. Then Liner thanked Stoyan and gave him a sealed envelope which he asked him to open at home. He stepped into the hotel and asked reception to get his bill ready for the morning. In his room he shaved, showered, poured himself half a glass of whisky and drank it in one go. Suddenly, he decided to take a walk around the city centre.

The boulevard took him to a small square full of young people. In the middle there was a monument depicting a priest gripping a cross and gazing at the sky. Liner continued down a narrow street next to a tramline. He reached a small, tidy market whose fruit and vegetable displays looked like a still life. On the right-hand side there was a church and a small park. He kept walking next to the tramline until he reached a large square with a cathedral on one side and a neon sign on a building saying Hotel Sheraton on the other. Liner went down into a subway in front of the Sheraton. He turned left and found himself in a well-lit passage with signs leading to the metro station. A blind man sat on the stone edge lining the passage wall. His hand gripped a small plastic cup with a few coins inside. The cup was tied to his single coat button. His eyes were white like those of a statue. He was singing some drawn-out, sorrowful song. Liner approached carefully and sat on the stone next to him. The man blinked – he must have sensed Liner's presence – but didn't interrupt his song. Passers-by cast shadows across the white marble of his eyes. The song was endless. Christopher Liner suddenly thought of his mother. His father had died, and she lived in the north of England where he went to see her at Christmas. But last Christmas he was busy and didn't go. She was always making something in cross-stitch, and kept wanting to give Christopher one of her works, and he always promised he'd take it with him next time. He reached in his pocket for money to give the blind man. But instead of money, he felt a piece of paper. He took it out and unfolded it. It was a sheet from a school notebook, with carefully drawn Cyrillic letters: А, Б, В, Г, … He remembered the child with the too-big jacket.

Christopher Liner stared at the letters. He had the feeling that these letters contained everything that had happened to him these last few days. А was like a big shepherd with a stick across his waist. Б like a praying girl. В like a mountain. Г like a gallows.

And suddenly, he remembered the name of that black-haired girl at the hotel. He remembered the name she'd told him, the name he'd repeated all night long. He looked around, his mouth slack, but in his shock he didn't see a thing. No, it was impossible. It had to be a bad joke. The worst joke imaginable.

When his eyesight returned, he saw that the blind man had gone.

About the Translator

KAPKA KASSABOVA was born and raised in Sofia before her family emigrated to New Zealand. She moved to the UK in 2004 and now lives in Edinburgh. She is the author of two volumes of poetry, *Someone Else's Life* and *Geography for the Lost*, both published by Bloodaxe Books, and the memoir *Street Without a Name*, published by Portobello Books.